The King of Afton Park

Van Guines

Inquiries and Book Orders should be addressed to:

Great Writers Media
Email: info@greatwritersmedia.com
Phone: 877-600-5469

ISBN: 978-1-959493-60-0 (sc)
ISBN: 978-1-959493-61-7 (ebk)

Acknowledgments

I would like to dedicate this book to Mary Jo Moton.

Sorry it took me so long.

I would like to thank Mike Huffaker for his technical assistance couldn't have done it without you.

My name is Shang Butler. I live in Chattanooga, Tennessee. I was sitting in front of Robert's barbershop on the shoeshine stand, it was about 2:30 p.m. on a Tuesday afternoon. The weather was warm; it hadn't gotten hot yet. Summer was just around the corner. I wasn't there for just a shoeshine. I was perched up there to keep a look out for Willie Green. He was a two-timing gambler, who had hit the number for $4,500 on Sunday evening. So there was a least three people looking for him besides me. First would be his wife of ten years, Thelma Green, and his two kids.

Then there would be a cat we called Pepsi Cola who was a well-known loan shark; he had been sitting in his car in front of Willie's house for a day and a half, but still no Willie. So he hired me to find Willie and collect whatever money Willie had left and bring his behind home. See, Pepsi

Cola was Thelma's uncle. The third person was a lady named Jessie, she was Willie's chick on the side. I had a feeling that she would see Willie before any of us would. She worked at the beauty parlor across the street. That's what I was waiting for. I looked down at my shoes that Melvin Jackson was hard at work shining.

Then I caught a glimpse of a vision of loveliness coming across the street. At the time, I didn't know she was coming my way. I had my eye out for Willie Green and all that loot he may have left after his disappearing act. As she came across the street, I realized that it was Mary Joe Morton, the grand-daughter of Mr. Tom Morton and Josephine Morton who owned most of the small businesses in Alton Park, where I now sat. Her mother, Sadie May Sublee, was married to Mr. Tom's son, Zeebdee, who was killed about a year ago.

She walked up to the shoeshine stand and said, "Good afternoon, may I have a word with you, sir?"

The Sublee family was always very polite, the women anyway. So I said, "Good afternoon to you. What's on your mind?"

I invited her to sit down, but there was no place else to sit but up in one of the shoeshine chairs, so she climbed up and sat right down. Being as her family owned everything in sight at the time, why not? I thought. She asked me if I had heard about the murder of her father. I nodded my head then removed my hat to show my condolences and respect. As she fought back a tear, she began to tell a story. She had gone to the Ball Park, which is what we folks in Chattanooga called the baseball diamond where the Negro leagues played.

Josh Gibson, Satchel Page, all the greats played there. She only lived two blocks away in a small neighborhood called Lincoln Park. I lived around the block from her family home myself. So I knew that she was on foot walking home after the ball game. She stopped talking and took a look around when she saw no one else but me and Melvin.

She said, "Melvin, I think I need a soda, would you like a soda, Mr. Butler?" She pulled out a dollar bill, but sodas were a nickel at the Smokehouse bar and grill that was just down Main Street right off Johnson Avenue.

Melvin took the dollar and said, "What flav you want, Miss Mary Joe?"

She said, "Orange will do fine. Please, get yourself something too."

He said, "Yes, ma'am" then took off down the street. When he got out of earshot, she took another look around, then she began to speak. She said that she was coming down O'Neal Street where there's an alley between O'Neal and Garfield Street and a man came out of the alley, he almost ran into her. When he saw who she was, he jumped back, fell to the ground, then he started to cry out "Please, forgive me." She wasn't sure who he was at first. Then after looking at him closely, she realized that it was the man they called Big John, the man who shot her father, Zeebdee, the man that the cops had let go, honoring his claim of self-defense, not even putting the handcuffs on the murderer.

As he got off the ground and climbed to his feet, he realized that this young woman could do him no harm, at least not at the moment anyway. She would have gone to sound the alarm, run a few blocks at least before her uncles and family could hear her. So Big John began to weep softly, at first he told her that he was sorry that he had shot her father. He said that he hasn't known not one second of peace since he was allowed to walk away from that bar that night. He looked really scared, like he had seen a ghost, the crying spell got worse; he spoke in jags and spurts, he kept saying that they wouldn't let it go.

"They wouldn't let it go. It was like he was talking to someone else now, like I wasn't even there." She stopped looked around again and said, "You know, Mr. Tom got a bounty on his head."

I said, "Last I heard it was $1,000. Do you want me to go find him?"

"Yes and no," she said. "I want to know who made him kill my daddy. If you find him and turn him over to the Morton Boys, that would end it without finding out who's behind all this. Someone made that man shoot my daddy. I want to know who and I want to know why." She let that fall between us.

When I looked at her face, I could see that she was very determined to get these answers that she wanted. She took out a fifty-dollar bill and said that she wanted to hire me to look into it for her, said that she would be working a summer job at Leggett's, one of the only stores that black folks like us were allowed to shop and work in the front part of the store where I'm sure she would be working. I didn't have much to say at first. I thought about Mr. Tom and how I heard he was really sick. I was wondering about that $1,000 reward. Then I started thinking about all the people who looked to cash in on that reward and had failed. Simply came back with nothing to show, no Big John. Now he's stumbling out of alleys right into the man's daughter for God's sake.

So I said, "Yeah, okay, Miss Maryjo."

She had to be at least eighteen years old. I heard she had gotten into Hampton Institute all the way up in Virginia. "Yeah, I will look into it, but I'm not going to take your money."

She said, "Why not and let the fifty just hang out there."

I said, "I don't want Toy and Pay hunting me down looking for your money back if I can't find Big John."

She said, "I think he's been living in the hobo town near the train tracks or down by Citico Creek. I think he's been right under our noses the whole time. That's why nobody's found him. Nobody would think a high roller like Big John would be hiding in hobo town. Well if he's down there, I'll find him. I have found many men hiding from the loan sharks and ex-wives or whoever." She put the fifty down by my hand, got up to meet Melvin coming back down the street with sodas. He put the big orange crush soda bottle in her hand then made a point to give her back her change. I guessed he didn't want to hear from Toy and Pay either. I've been finding people for years. I started right after WW1.

* * *

I was fifteen years old when the Tennessee colored Army reserve got the call to go to Europe, France to be specific. We started out digging ditches, like we did in and around Chattanooga. We started working with what is now the TVA (Tennessee Valley Authority), working on stopping the flooding from the Chattanooga and Citico Creeks.

Soon after we got to France, we were put in the 369 infantry in the ninety-third division. We were sent to the Argonne Forest around the end of April 1918. All the black troops were armed and outfitted well with the same gear the French troops were given. This was a first. We had never been given much of anything a white soldier had, unless he was done with it. So the first action I saw in this 191-day battle was on the twenty-first day, must have been the last day of April.

We were pinned down by machine-gun fire on one side of what must have been a big farm. At the edge of the forest, it was raining hard, so Col. Ballard and his command had taken cover in an old barn, safe from the machine-gun fire the officers had held up there. Soon as the rain stopped, we heard the far-off sounds of aircraft. It was then we saw a Sopwith Camel then another, they had English marks. They started dropping bombs on all the machine gun nest that had us pinned down. We started cheering, so we didn't hear the sound of the German planes. As they came over head, soon there was a dogfight. That's what they called it when planes took each other on. Pretty soon, the British planes forgot about the machine gun nests and were tied up in the dogfight. However, they did manage to quiet two out of the three gunners that were holding us down. We were able to move up to a trench near the barn.

Soon after that, one of the planes was hit. It started to smoke, then it started to lose altitude; we had no way to tell whether it was German or British, all we could see was smoke. The plane appeared coming in low from the west side of the barn. Next thing we knew, it hit the barn, and the whole thing went up in a cloud of smoke. Flames broke out.

We knew that the command was in the barn. As soon as we could, we ran to the big door on the far side of the barn to see if we could open the door. That's when the last of the enemy machine gunners woke up and started shooting, so we had to fall back. Soon we could hear men in the barn starting to yell out, some trying to escape, some burning and crying out for help.

I managed to get up near the big door, got it opened, and went inside. Even though it was on fire, the machine gunner couldn't seem to shoot inside the barn too well now that I look back on it, that must have been a 30 caliber. The British had knocked out the 50 caliber. When I got inside, I saw two men down on the ground near the door. I managed to grab them both by the collar and dragged them out of the barn. By that time, we had some men up by the barn with what we called a bar (browning automatic rifle) as they started shooting. I handed off my two and went back in the barn. I found two more men, one was on fire. I put out the fire, brought him out first, then went back for the others. All in all, we managed to get command and all his men out of the barn. Some were dead already, to make a long story short, Col. Ballard hated the black troops under his command, but everyone knew what had happened. Soon, word got back to the general, yeah, Black Jack himself heard about the battlefield barn rescue.

Shortly after that, I was made a corporal, fifteen years old. I was told to set up a squad of men that would be charge with retrieving wounded and dead soldiers from the battlefield during and after the battles, of course, the wounded came first over the dead. But it came down from command, some say Black Jack himself, that he wanted all his soldiers, black and white, to be retrieved from the battlefield alive or dead. If the latter, he wanted their belongings, money, letters, metals, etc. collected and sent back to the families in the states. This could be done through the black USO. So I was always seen going through the pockets of dead troops. Some called me a grave robber, my squad knew better. We got in a lot of fights because of our jobs. I was a big kid 6 feet tall, 190 pounds by then, and strong mostly from all that digging. So nobody would call me grave robber to my face. Meanwhile, all the men we rescued had nothing but praise for my squad and the medics we worked with.

On the 125th day of the 191-day battle of the Argonne Forest, we were trench hopping, that was what we called it when we could advance forward from trench to trench as we ran across the short spaces between the holes. By this time, we were seasoned soldiers. There were German soldiers still in the trench, we jumped in as machine-gun fire started up ahead of us. We fired our bolt action rifles at and into those men in the trenches. This was not the first time I had shot and killed the Kaiser's men. I saw the guy I shot fall as he did, I darn near landed on top of him. About this time, the other men in the hole started to react, some ran down the trench, others put their rifles up to use their bayonets; as this happened, I was stuck under my chin. A neck wound can be fatal on the battlefield. There was no time to react, we had to keep fighting. There were three Germans left, and we had lost two out of the five guys we came across the field with, so I drew my side weapon and fired it at the closest man to me. Then the medic we called Jon took his rifle up like a bat and hit one of the Germans in his head, I think it broke his neck when he spun around his rifle, fired a shot that hit our third man, killing him. The third German saw this all happened, turned, and started to run away. As he did, he tossed a grenade down in a rolling fashion. I grabbed the body of the German I had shot and flung his body at the rolling explosive, then we both dove away from it as it went off.

When the smoke from it cleared, Jon and I were both okay. A small amount of shrapnel in my arm and cuts to the side of the field doc's head, but we could hardly hear anything. We knew that there was still machine-gun fire overhead, but we could hardly hear it. Jon took a look at my face, and from his expression, I knew it was bad. I had blood all over the front of my uniform. Jon was a hell of a field doctor. He had made what he called a pressure wrap bandage on the battlefield one day. This had saved many of the men we had pulled off the battlefield. He stuck one of those under my chin then put some water on my arm to stop the burning from the shrapnel.

As we rested a few and our hearing came back, we knew that our time was running out. We had to get out of that hole quick. So we came up with a plan. We tossed the bodies of the remaining German soldiers up out of the trench. As we did, we used those bodies to cover our crawling retreat across the space we had come from; as we did, we managed to retrieve two of the three men we had lost. On our way to that trench, one soldier was still clinging to life. Needless to say, any neck or head injury will get you a boat ride home, the war for me was over. I spent weeks in the hospital in the black and French section. Jon had talked to the French doctors about me and made them do some kind of special operation on my face. I think today they called it cosmetic surgery. All I know was when I got my orders to leave the hospital, every man who could stand raise his arms or both saluted me as I walked out of door. When I got back to the states, I was only allowed in the black section of the Army base. Part of that area was the black USO building.

The first thing I saw was all the belongings of the dead soldiers from the battlefield I had shipped back. It seemed like there was no one to deliver them. As I looked in my belongings, I found the letter I had received on the battlefield. I was almost sure it came from General Black Jack's office. So I had one of the ladies from the USO office write me a letter to that office, telling them what was happening. About two weeks later, I was stuck around the base waiting on my discharge papers when a letter came back addressed to me. The Army had given me a full discharge, and I was sent a purple heart to go along with the two metals the French had given me on my way out the door. Then the letter said that I was to be hired to deliver all the belongings to the families or next of kin to all those black soldiers who had perished on the battlefield. If I took the job, I would be paid, plus the Army would cover my expenses. They had set up a system so every family I contacted would sign a letter, saying that they had received the belongings of their soldiers.

So I went about the business of traveling around the country, finding each soldier's family. Back in those days, it was bad for a black man to travel around the country. There were riots and lynchings of black WW1 vets going on all over the nation. So I traveled by bus. I did not walk around empty-handed, as we said on the battlefield. I had found a way to bring home any and all the small arms I could carry, any gun or knife we found in those trenches I kept it. I kept to myself as I would come into a town. I would stay in the black section of town. America was still very segregated. I found the best way to find a family in the black section, it was to go by the church or the black undertakers, either way they would always have some info or idea where the family could be found.

Once in New York, some bums tried to rob me, they took one look at my .45 caliber service revolver that I carried in my duffle bag and hauled ass. I ran across a lot of people down on their luck. Then one day, I got lucky and found me a good deal on a car. I still traveled around on the bus. If a black man would show up in town with his own car, it would draw to much attention. It took me about five years to deliver all the belongings. Near the end, I went to Mississippi. I saved stuff liked that in the deep south for last on purpose. I had three deliveries to make in that state. When I got to Tupelo, Mississippi, the undertaker in the town who handled the burying of black people was a white man. He had recently passed away himself. His kids who left Mississippi years ago where in the process of closing down his business. When I came by to see if I could get the info on the family I was looking for, they had no knowledge of the family. They had been gone so long they didn't know much about who was there anymore. They did have a hearse for sale. Darn fine-looking car. I gave them $110 for it. The big death wagon was almost new. The old man had taken real good care of the car. I drove it to my next and last stop. Nobody looked twice at me driving around in that car. I drove it back to Chattanooga and parked it around back side of my little house I owned on Garfield.

The house belonged to my grandmother who I had to go and live with when I was nine years old, my parents were killed in a house fire. My grandmother cleaned house for years for a very rich family named Brooks, they owned the candy company. As years went by, she helped raised the Brooks family's only son, Norton. Soon after he got out of college and started working for the company, his parents passed away. He moved into the big house and told my grandma that if she stayed on, she could have whatever she wanted. So he bought her the house from whoever owned it then helped her set it up so when she passed away, the house would belong to me. The house was small, just three big rooms. Then when I moved in, she had the back porch closed in to make a bedroom for me. We heated the house with wood. The stove we cooked on made more than enough heat. Now that the house was mine, I put in a wood stove and cooked on a hot plate. I still go out in what we call the woods in Lincoln Park and cut down trees for firewood.

Once I returned home and resigned from my Army commission, I was able to save up my money and turn that car I bought into a taxi. I got an idea, I put the word out in all the small town local black newspaper and churches about the hearse. I was shocked at first when that telephone I had put in the house began to ring, it was undertakers from all around the state calling to find out if they could rent the hearse. I would drive it around from town to town and made pretty good money. Then as I got settled into a living-working routine, I started to enjoy life in Chattanooga.

My grandma had a big vegetable garden, I grew most of the food I eat. I spend most of my mornings working in the garden or cutting wood. I found some men clearing a lot a block from my house, I talked them into dumping all the trees on the empty lot next door to my house, I built me a fence. Then I got me a dog, named him Black Jack, built him a doghouse, then used the rest for firewood. In the evening, I would drive my cab. I would pick up the working folks, then as night would fall, I started driving around the high rollers. They dressed nice and spent all night going around the Chattanooga black underworld. So I fell right in line with them. I would come out three or four in the afternoon, put my clothes on, get on the cabstand on Main Street owned by Mr. Tom, then after driving an hour or two, I would stop into places like Miss Sadie's place, Maryjo's Mama's place, where people like Pepsi Cola, Bill Kent, Pap and Bean Gaines, and tough guys like Maryjo's uncles, Toy and Pay Sublee, and many others hung out.

Folks would get in my cab with problems. I would look into it if they made it worth my while. I didn't charge much to help folks who didn't have much. Then the loan sharks got wind of the fact that I knew how to find people, that I was in the Great War, I was nobody to play around with. They paid me a percentage of whatever it was they were able to collect from the folks that owed them. Now even though there was a depression, there was work in the pipe foundries and slaughter yards. Hell, now and then, they would hire black people at the Tennessee Valley Authority then, so the clubs and speakeasies like the Smokehouse were goldmines.

Mr. Tom had come to Chattanooga from New Orleans. He worked his way north to Tennessee on the railroads, I was told. He got a job cooking downtown for one of the big hotels. That's where he learned to cook those big meals he would fix and sell to all the men who worked at the pipe factory and the slaughterhouse where he bought his meat. That was during the day. At night, he opened up the back room for gambling, just crap games at first then he added on to the building and opened upstairs and closed in the back room. There were high stakes card games and high rollers from all over the south. He started running his own numbers racket, which got noticed from the Dixie mob. They controlled the numbers racket for the black and white Chattanooga underworlds. I was told that Mr. Tom had his own connection through New Orleans. Mr. Tom's sister, Mattie Lee Morton, was married to New Orleans mobster Bobby Ganno, who married Mattie Lee in spite of the New York mobs' objection. You see, Mattie Lee and Mr. Tom were Creoles. If you ever saw Mr. Tom, he looked a lot like the little Jewish men I saw when I was in Europe. Bobby Ganno was born and raised in New Orleans. Some say that his dad had housekeepers that were Creoles. They raised Bobby so that when his daddy got cancer and died, Bobby took over the New Orleans racket. He paid his dues to the New York mob, but he cared less about their approval. If you saw Mattie Lee, you would think that she was a white woman.

Mattie ran a nightclub called The Gate that Bobby G. owned. The Gate was the biggest nightclub in New Orleans. Mattie would get the numbers off The New York Times newspaper in the morning then call Tom every day by noon with the numbers. The Dixie mob didn't get the numbers till that evening when the train arrived, so Mr. Tom had the jump on them.

The Dixie mob didn't like it one bit. The boys in New York had little to say. See, the Dixie mob was ran by a guy they called the Lizard. His name was Lenny Lazzario. He was sent to Chattanooga when he was seventeen years old. His dad, who they say was some kinda underboss in one of the mob families, I forgot which, was killed in a car wreck. He was hit by a drunk driver, his driver and bodyguard, Max Lucci, killed the drunk driver with his bare hands, broke his neck, and just left him behind the wheel of his car. They say that the mob wasn't sure what to do with Lenny, I guess they kinda owed him, so they sent him down to Chattanooga with Max Lucci to set up the rackets here in Chattanooga, out of sight, out of mind. But with the guidance of Max and the willingness to hurt or kill anyone that got in their way, they managed to make a go out of the Chattanooga black and white rackets. That is northeast and west of town.

They even had the black gangsters in St. Elmo, which was on the southwestern part of town and stood in the shadow of Lookout Mountain. Those men were controlled by two cousins, Pap and Bean Gaines. They were the best dressed, sharpest, most dapper crooks in all of Chattanooga and some of the most dangerous men in town; they would be at all the black clubs, even the Smokehouse. I was told that they tried to put the bite on Mr. Tom for Lenny the Lizard, but Tom's men were ready. Then there's the crooks to the east. That would be Bill Kent, a numbers man who controlled all the numbers in the black section of an area we called Glenwood, he joined up with Lenny's mob a few years ago. Now it was said that he had men writing numbers all the way out to east Brainard.

At one time it was said that Bill Kent and Sadie Mae had a fling. Sadie Mae, being married to Zeebdee, Mr. Tom's son, was a real indication of the gall a man like Bill Kent had. Sadie Mae was a fine woman, all right, but I don't know if I would want to risk my neck dating a lady with dangerous baggage like that. Hell, just the fact that Zeebdee ran around with men like her brothers Toy and Pay was enough to give, even a war veteran like me, a chill. Miss Sadie owned and ran a club a called Sadie Mae's which was on Main Street in Alton Park. It was the biggest and best nightclub in the black section of Chattanooga; she had jazz bands and music shows and plays come to town to put on a show at her place. Big stars like Jelly Roll Morton, Fats Domino, Muddy Waters, and Little Walter came to the club several times a year. I was told that Mr. Tom and Jelly Roll Morton may have been related, one thing for sure he never came to town and not come by the Smokehouse after hours. I've seen him there myself many times.

Sadie's brother, Pay, ran security for the club. He was in the Great War too. He was a welder, he was there when we got off the ship in Europe. Now the day time, he worked at the pipe foundry, and most nights, he was at Sadie's. I was told that there was a break in at the club two or three times. So Pay waited all night in the kitchen near the window were the thieves were coming in. When the window slid open and the thief put his hands up on the windowsill to pull himself into the window, Pay took a sharp butcher's knife and stuck it through the man's hand. Then as he screamed and bled, Pay cut on the light so he could see his face. Pay told him that if he ever broke into Sadie's place again, he would kill him. Let's just say that there hasn't been a break in since.

Toy was Pay's younger brother, he ran and handled the numbers for Mr. Tom. He was known for a time when Tom first got started with numbers, some of the boys from St. Elmo tried to rob Toy. He was able to out draw and shoot both men. Some say that these men were from the Pap Gaines's gang. I never was sure. All this information was common knowledge in the black underworld of Chattanooga. Toy and Zeebdee worked and ran all the numbers and outside rackets for Tom. The inside operation was oversaw by one of Tom's nephews, a huge man they called li'l Jake who lived in a big room Tom had put in when he had the upstairs built. Jake ran the gambling, oversaw the ladies who worked the bar and grill area. He also handled any trouble that took place inside the club. He carried a sawed-off shotgun he called old Betsy. He had several cousins and brothers, they were known as the Morton boys. Mr. Tom just called them his boys. It must have been seven or eight of them. They did Toy and Zeebdee's bidding. They had sisters and wives, they all worshiped and worked for Mr. Tom and his family.

* * *

Tom's brother, Robert, owned the barbershop and the shoeshine stand where I now sit. He and Tom had set up a cabstand out in front of the grocery store, the swap stand, and the farmer's market. This made jobs and opportunities for other men and women in the black community. Hell, I had a cab out there myself. The cabstand was run by a man named Henry. We called him Mr. Henry, he oversaw the cabstand, collected the fees, and settled any beef between the drivers or their passengers. He was in World War 2. He was a short, dark-skinned man, very wide and strong. I've seen him pick up a grown man and toss him 10 feet. His full-time job seemed to be to drive Miss Josephine, Mr. Tom's wife. Most folks called her Miss Josie, she had several beauty parlors around Alton, Lincoln, and Highland Park which were the areas that Toy and Zeebdee and the Morton gang controlled. Mr. Henry drove her around all day to collect the booth rent on all the chairs in the shops, manage the shops, buy the supplies, and settle any disputes between the ladies, and I heard there were many.

A lot of the Morton boys' wives and their daughters worked at the shops. That always led to some kind of friction. They said that Josephine could silence any arguments with just one look. I heard she carried a gun and a knife in her purse. She had a handful of big diamond rings that would cut skin with the slightest blow. Mr. Henry would take her back and forth to pick up all that cash. Nobody knew where it all went. Back then after the depression, nobody trusted banks.

Now those were some of the players in the game. I had sat here a while, so I got back in my cab to sit on the cabstand, hoping to pick up a fare. Soon a lady came out of the beauty parlor. She got in my cab and said, "Take me to 2600 McCallie Street."

As I turned around to see her face, it was Jessie Jamison, Willie Green's chick on the side. She turned her pretty head to look out the window as I pulled away from the curb. She had no idea I was looking for Willie. I was willing to bet good money that she was headed for a meet right now. The address was at the corner of McCallie and Dobbs Street, it was a nice, big apartment building at one time. Now it was what looked like a flophouse.

She got out and paid my fare, took up her bags, which I didn't see at first, it looked like groceries. Now I knew that she was headed for a meet up with Willie Green. So I pulled away like I was leaving, turned on Dobbs Street, and pulled up on the far side of the building. I could actually see both sides of the building's any comings and goings. By me being in the cab, nobody would have thought twice about me sitting there. While I sat there, I thought about Maryjo and her run in with Big John. To think that all the Morton boys were looking for him since he shot and killed Zeebdee. I remembered reading in the newspaper that Officer W. B. Robinson had investigated and called the shooting self-defense. John claimed that Zeebdee hit him with a pool stick. Zeebdee loved to play pool. He and his daddy had opened up three pool halls in Alton and Highland Park. Zeebdee was one of the best pool sharks in all of Chattanooga. He almost always carried a gun and had Toy or Pay and a host of the Morton boys around. Why in the world would he be over in Avondale playing pool by himself? That's just one more thing that didn't add up.

I would have to ask Maryjo, it may be better if I could talk to Toy or Pay, I'm sure they knew what he was doing there. Soon I got a break. I saw Jessie come back out and stand in front of the building. Soon a new car pulled up, a 1950 Chevrolet; she got in, leaned over, then sat back as the car pulled off. I wasn't ready for that. By the time I got the cab started and turned around, the car was blocks up the street. A traffic light on McCallie Street caught me, and I lost sight of the car as it went up McCallie to the intersection at Kelley Street, looked like they headed toward Glenwood when I lost sight of the car.

I turned left on Kelley Street and headed toward Highland Park to check in with Pepsi Cola, he was still hold up outside the house. Thelma had come out and brought him some dinner. I told him what I saw and where I had dropped off Jessie. He didn't like the sound of the new Chevrolet. He said that we better find him quick or he won't have a dime to take care of them babies and Thelma, who I'm sure was worried by now. The man been gone for three days now. I told him that I would stay on it. We left it at that. So I headed home to eat dinner and feed my dog, Black Jack; he liked to eat at night.

When I got near the house, I thought about Maryjo, her family lived in Lincoln Park on Pierce Street around the corner from my house. My grandmother and her grandma used to be friends. They used to share things out of the garden. Mama Sublee was what we used to call her. That's how I know so much about Mr. Tom's early days. So I rode past the house, hoping to see the young lady out front or on the block coming back from the corner store. I wouldn't dare stop to knock on the door. A man my age at the door asking after an eighteen-year-old young woman would not go over well. I would have Toy and Pay at my throat before I could explain a thing, let alone a look from Mama Sublee. I think that would hurt worse.

I didn't see Maryjo, so I went to my house. Like I said, it's a small house with a little front yard like most the houses in this neighborhood. I had space on the right side of house, so I made that my driveway. I was able to park the cab beside the hearse. Then I went in to warm up my dinner, I had made me a mess of collard greens and kale from out of my garden. I always put them over some corn bread and pour a bit of the juice over them. We called that pot liquor. I had a small bit of ham in there. I had made some mint tea from the mint plants that grew in my garden. I put that on the stove to warm and opened up my back door. When I looked outside, Black Jack was heading toward the back door. Tail wagging, he was a big dog, a mix between a black Labrador and German shepherd. He's been here for seven years. Now it's his backyard as well as mine. Now that I got the fence up, he can have the run of the place. He finally learned to stay out of my garden, so we get along just fine. I fed him then ate my dinner. After I showered and shaved, I put on my white tailor-made shirt I had made by Miss Moody, she was the best black tailor in town. She had a shop up on Main Street, it was said that Mr. Tom helped her buy the house she had lived in and made into her shop. Then I put on my blue plaid slacks and my blue shoes then my spats. I still had my dress spats from the Army. They still looked good as new. Once I put on my light blue sport coat, I headed out.

I drove past Mama Sublee's house, hoping to see Maryjo walking to the store. I got lucky and saw her walking down the street toward the corner store. I pulled up ahead of her to the curb. She walked up on the passenger side of the cab.

I said, "Good evening, I was hoping to see you. I have a few questions about your case before I can move forward."

She stopped and looked up the block toward the house and said, "Good evening to you, Mr. Shang. What questions do you have, sir?"

"Well for one thing, I want to know why your dad was playing pool in an area so far away from home. Don't he and Tom own two or three pool halls in Alton Park?"

She turned her head to look up the street again then said, "Actually, they own five if you count the two in Highland Park, one on the corner of Dobbs and Twenty-Eighth Street, and the other one is in the 2100 Block of Main Street, so I don't know why he was playing pool way over in Avondale all by himself."

I said, "Where was Toy and Pay, where were the Morton boys?"

She said, "I asked Toy, but he won't talk to me. He's afraid I'll tell my mama what he says and she will get mad. Pay was out of town at the time." Then she said, "I asked Mr. Tom."

When she paused, I said, "How is Mr. Tom?"

She looked down and said, "He's got kidney stones real bad. He's in a lot of pain. The doctors said he only has one kidney left, and that one is failing him."

I said, "I'm sorry to hear that."

Then she looked away as tears rolled down her cheeks, then she said, "I love Mr. Tom. I asked him if he knew why my dad was there, and he said dam if he knew. He said Daddy was real sad about a week before he was killed. Then a few days before the murder, he got real glad again, so Tom thought everything would be all right. Mr. Tom said that he thought that only Sadie Mae could get his boy down like that 'cause when my mama gets mad, there's no thunderstorm I've ever seen could keep up."

Then I said, "Do you think Toy would talk to me?"

She looked down the street again then said, "I was hoping you would go find Big John. He got to know who's behind all this."

Then I said, "I will look for him soon, but it would help to know why Zeebdee was there. Something seems kinda fishy."

She said, "I'll call Toy when I go back in the house. I know he'll be at club Sadie May tonight."

I said, "Okay, where's Pay?"

She smiled and said, "Pay is out of town. Toy and I took him to the airport yesterday evening, he flew to Chicago on his way to Seattle, Washington." She turned to walk away and said she would take care of it.

I said, "Thanks, I'll let you know when I round up Big John."

As I pulled away, I wondered what would I do with the killer if I could find him. Would he drop to his knees, or will he leap for my throat like one of the Kaiser's men? Hard to say till then. My next thought was about that $1,000 bounty. With Mr. Tom laid up in a sickbed, who would be the one to pull out that kinda cash? Hell, I've seen some of the Morton boys beat a guy half to death for a $50 slight. I couldn't see li'l Jake putting down old Betsy long enough to fork over the cash. No, Mr. Tom was a man of his word, but he's out of action right now and sounds like at his age maybe for good. This was a bridge best crossed when I came to it.

Meanwhile, I had to go by and pick up my girl. Doris was my main girl, she and I have been dating for a year or so. She worked at the Piggly Wiggly on Chamberlain Street in Highland Park. It was one of the nicest grocery stores in the black community, it was owned like most of the grocery stores in black Chattanooga by a Jewish fellow by the name of Simon Goldstein. Simon liked me, and he was a good boss to Doris. She managed the front of the store and all the cashiers, he liked me to come by the store with the cab so his elderly customers could get a cab ride home with their bags. I helped him set up a cabstand, and when I had time, I would manage it, and in exchange, he and Doris would take the phone calls that came in from people in other towns who wanted the services of the hearse or needed any detective work, this was a fair trade. I put down that phone number in my newspaper ad, added as a message number.

When I pulled up, Doris was coming out of the door. She was always ready to roll when she got off work. She lived across the street from the store, so if we had a date, she would go home during her lunch hour and get ready. She had on a cute blue dress, it fitted her tight brown frame so well. We would always plan our next date on the date we were on at the time. We would call out a color, tonight was blue night obviously. She got in the car, gave me a hug and a kiss, then said, "You kinda late, what's going on?"

She knew that the Army had drummed punctuality into me long ago. She was a brown-skinned woman, around thirty-four years old. She had been married to a fellow who went off to war in WW2 and didn't come back. She had a round face with big brown eyes and a wide African-looking nose. She smiled a lot which in my book made her a good-looking woman. Sometimes if I would leave her alone too long when we went out to a club, I would come back to our table and there would be some cat standing there, pleading his case. Doris was always pleasant but firm. So most of the time, they would move on without any trouble. I told her about the Willie Green thing first. She knew Jessie from high school. I don't think she liked that girl.

She said, "You mean to tell me Jessie James, the man stealer, was in this cab with you today and you ain't already between her legs? Well this Willie Green must show nuff have his ass some loot going then."

I guess she had a point about Jessie, Thelma Green was sure her best witness. I didn't tell her about finding the killer for Maryjo yet. We would get around to that soon. She knew a lot of the Morton boys and girls, she had been to the Smokehouse and Sadie Mae's with me and without me many times. She got her hair done at one of Josephine's beauty parlors for years and had seen Mrs. Morton in action a few times. Most of the info I have of the battles in the shops came from Doris, so we went back to Alton Park to club Sadie so we could snag us a good table. The club was slow, so we were able to get us some good seats. We liked to sit back away from the stage. Tonight, they had a local band, which was not unusual for a Tuesday. It was a five-man jazz band, a sax, two guitars, a drummer, and a cat on the piano; they didn't sound too bad. I liked jazz.

Soon a waitress came to the table and took our drink orders. Doris liked rum and coke. I had a beer but just let it sit there. As far as I was concerned, I was still working. We got up to dance a few times, then I saw Toy walked in the room from the kitchen. He came out, took a look at the room, then he leaned on the bar and ordered a beer. Sadie Mae came out, she looked around the room too. She saw Toy by the bar and came over and said a few words then went out into the room to talk to the waitresses. About that time, Toy looked in my direction. He pushed off the bar and headed toward our table. I could see from the look on his face that he was not pleased.

Toy was a slim fellow, very light-skinned like his sister, Sadie. He had a narrow face that I have never seen smile. His head was bald, but he always wore a hat. When he got to the table, he looked at me, but he spoke to Doris as he walked up to the table. Then he looked at me with a frown and said, "Maryjo told me you working on finding Big John."

I said nothing, just nodded my head. Doris's eyes got bigger as she looked at Toy then back at me. I waited him out because I didn't know what his young niece had told him about her run-in with Big John.

He said, "You want to know about Zeebdee? Man, this ain't no good time to talk."

I said, "Yeah, I know you a busy man."

He nodded his narrow head then said, "Meet me outside in back in ten minutes. I got to wait for Sadie May to leave." Then he looked around the room, I guess to see where Sadie was. He headed toward the kitchen.

After a few seconds, Doris looked like she was going to explode. So I told her to let it out. She gave a big exhale then said, "Man, this ain't no Willie Green-Jessie James case you gots to fill me in, that Zeebdee murder was a real humdinger. You looking for Big John? You think you gonna get that $1,000? I heard Mr. Tom was real sick. Where do you think Big John is at after all this time?"

I shook my head then stood up to leave 'cause by now it was time for my meeting out back with Toy. As I said before, Toy was not a man to fool around with. He always had a gun and a knife in his pocket. I looked over at the door just in time to see Sadie walk toward the door, I saw a man open the door for her, he had his head turned. As the door opened, I saw who it was. It was Bill Kent. As she walked out the door, she put her arm out, and he took it and led her toward the big Caddy that was parked at the curb. As they drove away, I walked around the side of the club into the alley.

Toy was leaning on his Ford. He looked up as smoke from the cigarette he was smoking rolled around his face. He said, "Man, this ain't no good time for you to be snooping around here."

I waited a beat then said, "I'm not snooping, just helping Maryjo."

He started nodding his head no.

I said, "I just got a few questions."

Toy's face turned even more sour. He sat back and said, "Like what?"

"Why was Zeebdee alone shooting pool in Avondale when the man owns five pool halls on his own turf?"

Toys mouth turned up at the corners for just a brief second, and that would be the closest to a smile I ever seen on the man's face. He said, "Look, man, this ain't your business. You gonna dig into a deep hole now."

"So why won't you tell Maryjo what happened that night. She lost her daddy, she got the right to know what caused it."

He looked down the alley toward the street. As he turned his head back toward me, I saw him reach behind his back. Then the gun was just right there in his hand. I never saw anybody move that quick. I stepped back to get out of his line of fire, but the gun won't for me. As I turned to look, I saw the problem. There were two men coming down the alley fast. They slowed their roll when they saw the gun. Toy looked at them with that sour look of his, and they stopped dead in their tracks. The two men were dressed to kill, they had on suits, hats, and some real shiny shoes.

The closest one to us said, "Toy, you know what Pap want, he gonna need an answer about that Smokehouse action."

Toy looked at him spit on the ground then said, "Do I look like Mr. Tom, fool?"

Then the other man looked at me. He said, "You lost, reaper."

I took a step toward him, and the other man came forward. As he moved, he cut across his buddy's path. I took that space between us in one step. As I did, I hit him with both my hands as hard as I could on his shoulder. When the blow hit him, he rocked back and fell into his buddy. As he did that, I just kept coming forward. I hit him in his face as he tried to keep his balance, then he and his buddy went down. Now both men lay on the ground. As I stood over them, they both began to reach for weapons. As the first man pulled his gun, I was able to snatch it from him. About that time, the one I pushed pulled out a razor. I took his arm and twisted it till I heard a sharp cracking sound. He cried out and rolled away. Now both men were still down. I grabbed them both, pulled them up; as they came to their feet, I pushed them both toward the front of the alley. When they stopped moving forward and went to turn around, I pulled the man's pistol that I had stuck in my belt when I had relieved him of it. Then they took two steps backward when they stopped. Toy stepped up beside me and put his gun up in their faces.

As they turned to run, Toy said to me, "No, don't shoot, not tonight, this ain't no good night for that."

We just stood there till they got in the car. As they pulled out, I heard the first man say "This ain't over, Toy" and then the other, "I'll see you again, reaper."

We just stood there and let those words fall to the ground. I looked at Toy, he gave me a head nod, and we moved toward the front door. He said, "I heard it won't no good idea to call you no reaper."

I nodded then looked up the street then said, "Those Pap's men, I take it, they still after the Smokehouse club?"

Toy frowned and said, "Not the club, they want the numbers. You know we got the numbers game all sewed up. We get the numbers so early Lenny and them can't keep up. Hell, we done paid off the winner, and he broke before they even know what the dam number is that day. Everybody in town want to play Tom's game. The lizard, Pappy, and that dam Bill Kent all want a bite out of that apple."

I said, "Sounds like y'all got your hands full."

Toy said, "Look, man, I don't run Sadie May, Sadie May run me. Ever since I was a baby."

I knew then what he meant. When Toy was a baby, Sadie and her sister, Nona, would drag Toy around all day, being he was the last of the twelve Sublee children. Those two sisters would spend time babysitting him. So folks in the neighborhood started calling him their toy baby doll since most little girls their age had toy dolls instead of a real baby to tote around. Now the name Toy is what he goes by.

I looked at him and said, "Do you think the numbers game got Zeebdee killed?"

Toy just shook his head and said, "Let's get out of this alley."

I followed him back inside. I wasn't going to get any more out of Toy that night. As I walked back to the table, I saw a man sitting on my seat. As I stepped up, I saw who it was, Bean Gaines was there talking to Doris. She saw me and took the smile off her face. Most men around town would get up as soon as I walked to the table. Bean stayed seated for a beat or two then said to Doris, "Well it was good to see you again."

As he got to his feet, he looked me up and down then nodded his head in an approving fashion. The man was dressed to kill, he had on a seersucker suit that was pink and white. The shirt he had on had to be tailor-made, it had a pink collar and was white at the body, the cuffs were pink. The collar had Bean on one side and Gaines on the other in small, real fancy letters. He had on some kinda gators, they were two tone, pink and white.

As he saw me looking, he smiled an evil grin of gold teeth and said, "You know, Miss Moody can put your name on them shirts you buy'n, you got to spend a bit more, but you on the right track may as well take the ride all the way up the incline. All the boys from St. Elmo had funny incline jokes since they lived in the shadow of Lookout Mountain. The home of the incline."

I nodded my head and took a step by him and took my seat. He tipped his white straw hat and stepped away. When he walked toward the bar, I saw one of the men at the bar step forward and say a few words to him. He looked our way again and grinned his evil grin. As he pulled up to the bar, two women came up to him; as he spoke to them, he took the money they handed him. He turned to the bartender, ordered something, and put his arms around both ladies. I turned to Doris who had her eyes on me.

She said, "What happen to you?"

I must have been gone too long. I said, "I'll tell you later."

When the band finished up, we got to our feet and headed to the door. When Toy saw us leaving, he headed to the door. He opened the door as we walked up. He stepped out and looked around. About that time, Toy's girlfriend, Tootsie, came up behind us, she was carrying a big bag, like a suitcase. Toy held the door for us as we stepped out on to the sidewalk. I heard her tell Toy, "That's all of it." They cut around the side of the club, and we walked to my cab. Two ladies were standing near the passenger's side of the car. They saw Doris and spoke up.

They asked, "Could we pay you to take us to Highland Park? We don't want to take no chances with the bus."

Doris smiled, she knew that if she wasn't with me, I would say sure, but I said, "Sorry, ladies, this cab is off duty."

One of the ladies looked mad, but she held her tongue. Doris gave me her "why not" look. So I said, "Where to, ladies?"

They gave me an address off McCallie, which was real near that flophouse I took Jessie James to. As we pulled away, I saw Toy and Tootsie pulled out of the alley and headed down Main Street toward Central. Once we got the ladies out of the car, I told Doris about the building near where we were.

She said, "Let's ride by there, we may see something."

As we pulled up to the corner of McCallie and Dobbs where the building was, we saw the new Chevy parked right there at the curb. When I looked around, I saw one of the cars Pepsi Cola drove. I got out and tapped on the car window; Pepsi was sitting in the driver's seat with his head down, he had his .38 long nose pistol on his lap. When I saw the gun, I took a sidestep to avoid getting shot by a startled loan shark, and show enough, he came awake, grab the gun, put it to the window, and pulled the hammer back.

I moved again and shouted, "It's me, Shang, Pepsi."

He looked up as he put the hammer down and lowered the gun.

I asked, "How long you been here?"

He said, "What time is it?" I told him it was midnight. He said, "I got here at 7:00 p.m."

I said, "Was that Chevy parked there then?"

He took a look and said, "Hell no, I musta slept through it when he pulled up."

I said, "We don't know for sure that's Willie's car, least not yet."

He said, "You told me somebody picked up that Jessie girl here this afternoon after you dropped her off. Who else could it be?"

I said, "I don't know, but we got to find out before you blow some fool's head off when they come out here to go to work in the morning."

I went to the door of the flophouse, opened it up, and looked in, there were six units downstairs and most likely six upstairs. I closed the door and went back to the car. I told Doris of my plan. She hopped out of the car, eager to participate. I came up to Pepsi's window and told him the plan. When I was ready, I gave Doris the signal, then I picked up two big, empty liquor bottles. I threw them to the ground over, near the Chevy. When they broke, it was loud, real loud.

About that time, Doris flung the door open and said in her loud, big voice, "Look, somebody stealing that new Chevy. They done broke the window."

As soon as she said that, I saw a light come on under the door in the first unit at the top of the steps. I heard voices, a man and a woman. About that time, I traded places with Doris by the door. When I got there, I heard footsteps coming down the stairs. When the door flew open, I saw Willie Green pop out of the door with something in his hand. I waited till he got clear of the door. I hit him on the side of his head, he must have been drunk 'cause he spun around and just sat down. I took the knife out of his hand, grabbed him by his arm, and lifted him to his feet. He looked worried till he looked up and saw Pepsi coming up the walkway. I stopped Willie in front of him, and Pepsi slapped Willie on the back of his head. Willie looked really sad and said, "How you find me, Shang?"

Before I could say anything, the door to the flophouse opened, and Jessie stepped out. She looked at me then at Pepsi and said, "What the hell is going on out here? Why you got your hands on my man? Have you lost your mind?" About that time, Doris, who I had almost forgotten about, said, "Your man, your man, you ain't never had a man in your life, girl, that won't with somebody else at the time.

Bitch, you ain't got no man. Jessie James, the man stealer."

When she heard that, she spun around. I could see that she was drunk. Doris didn't wait, she walked up to Jessie and slapped the woman. Jessie hit her back, they squared off and began to throw blows. Doris had told me once that when she was in high school, she ran track and played on the girls basketball team. She was very quick and strong, she grabbed the woman, picked her up, and tossed her to the ground. She shouted, "Your man stealing days 'bout over, girl."

When that happened, the door to the flophouse came open, and five or six folks came flinging out, shouting, "Fight, fight, fight."

I spent some time at Lincoln High myself before I went to the big war. I thought that I was back in sixth grade. I went to break up the fight and took my eye off Willie and Pepsi. I got my arms around Doris and picked her up. As I did, she kicked and screamed, she was clearly out of control, she had a few drinks at the club too, I remembered. I carried her toward the cab.

When I looked up, I saw Willie pulling away from the curb in a hurry. I looked for Pepsi, he was running to his car. When I put Doris down, she jumped at the girl again. I grabbed her arm and said, "Let's go."

She looked at me and took a breath, then she looked around at the crowd and said, "You got what was coming to you this time, bitch. Now let's see you steal another man."

Jessie got to her feet, you could see that the woman was wobbly, she staggered out toward the street and screamed, "Willie, where my willie?" She saw that the car was gone, she turned around and headed back up the walkway. She told Doris, "You lucky I'm drunk. I see you again, it gonna go bad for you."

Doris laughed, put a sneer on her face, and said, "You just let me know when you ready."

Jessie staggered forward into the building. The crowd followed her.

I ran down the walkway to see if they were still going down Dobbs. I could see the taillight of a car about six blocks up, no way to tell which car was which. I got Doris in the car and drove away. I went straight to her house to drop her off, thinking she might be mad with me for stopping her victory. She said nothing on the short ride home.

When we pulled up, she said, "How about the Smokehouse for dinner Saturday?"

And I said, "Okay, green be cool."

She nodded her head, kissed my cheek, and stepped out of the car. I watched her go in her apartment then drove home. I just couldn't believe Willie got away. I took a long shower, then lay down on my bed in what used to be my grandmother's room. When I finally got to sleep, I found myself back on the battlefield in the Argonne Forest. There were men fighting and dying all around me. I saw a wounded soldier lying in the mud with blood all around him, he saw me and reached out for me. Then I heard him say, "Reaper, reaper, don't leave me, don't let me die, reaper." I tossed and turned, trying to get away from that horrible scene.

I woke up covered in sweat. I was glad that I took Doris home so she wouldn't see how bad these dreams were when they came. I got up and showered again. I looked out the back door, and Black Jack was running around the yard barking. He never gets worked up like that unless somebody has been in the yard or near the fence. I picked up one of the guns I had on my gun shelf and walked out the back door. I didn't see anybody near the back fence, I walked to the side of the house, then I saw it or I heard it first, sirens, then I saw the smoke to the southeast of the house. Whatever it was burning, it was burning bad.

So it was almost midmorning. I got dressed in my early afternoon clothes, that's my tan knit slacks, my brown Stacy Adams shoes, and one of my brown-and-tan knit shirts. Now I was ready for cabstand duty. I could go by the market where Doris worked or go to the cabstand on Main where I was yesterday. I chose the stand on Main Street because I hoped to see Pepsi and find out if he caught up with Willie Green.

When I pulled up, I knew that something was wrong, people were standing around everywhere. There was smoke and ashes blowing around in the air. I got out the car and saw Melvin standing on top of his shoeshine stand. I walked over.

He looked down from the stand and said, "It burn down all the way to the ground."

I looked down the street but couldn't see much, so I said, "What's burning, Melvin, what is it?"

He jumped down off the stand, looked at me sadly, and said, "Sadie May's, it's gone all gone."

I said, "Dam, we were there last night. It must have burned down after midnight."

Melvin got up early, the man had a paper route, so he's out on street at four to five o'clock in the morning. He said, "It had to be after four this morning when it started 'cause when I came down Main Street. There won't nobody around. Well one thing for sure, won't nobody in there at that time."

I stepped back to my cab, leaned on the door. While I waited there, I saw people starting to go inside the buildings, not much else to see, not much else to say about it. After about thirty minutes, I got a few short fares from Main Street in to places in Highland Park, so I stopped at the cabstand on Chamberland Avenue at the Piggly Wiggly where Doris worked. I saw her inside the store through the front window. When she looked up and saw me, she smiled then waved. I waved back, then Simon saw me, he waved too. Then he came out to the cabstand and walked up to the driver's side window.

He said, "How are you?"

I said, "I'm fine, how's our girl doing today?"

He looked inside the window and said, "She seems sad today. Did something happened between you two? I hate to pry, but God forbid something happens to you two. I have nothing but love and respect for you both."

I looked out at him from the car window and said, "No, we are okay. She just got something on her mind."

He said, "Good, I have a favor to ask."

I said, "Okay."

He said, "Man never agree to a favor till you know what it is." He laughed then told me that he had a customer who was ill, she needed medicine and food delivered, she lived in Glenwood. He said, "She's a white lady, a Jew like me. She won't mind if you bring her things in the house." He said, "She would pay me on the spot. She has credit with him, she was okay."

I said, "Okay, write down the address so I can read it."

He laughed and said, "What you trying to say, you can't read my chicken scratch." I laughed too.

I took the packages to the house. On the way back from Glenwood, I passed by a diner at the corner of Glenwood Drive and Robbins Road. As I slowed for the traffic light, I saw a man standing by a car. He was a short, white man wearing a black suit on a hot day like this, he caught my attention. When I looked closer, I recognized him as Max Lucci, Lenny the Lizard's hit man. Soon as the light changed, I pulled over just to see what happened next. As I sat there a few minutes, I noticed a car in the lot that looked familiar. I wasn't sure where I had seen it. Then it hit me. That was Bill Kent's Caddy. I thought that I would give it a few more minutes. After about fifteen more minutes, I saw what I was waiting to see. Bill Kent came out of the diner behind Sadie May, she was walking fast, and she didn't look happy. I saw Kent grab her arm, then she pulled away. Some hot words were exchange, and she took a few steps toward the curb. I was hoping that she would need a cab. As soon as she got to the curb, Bill Kent came up behind her and said something to her that made her turn around. Then she headed for his Caddy's passenger door, she pulled it open and got in. Kent went around to the driver's side and got in.

It struck me odd that her nightclub burned down and she was way over here in Glenwood. As they pulled out, I saw the Lizard walk out of the diner around to the back door of the Caddy that Max Lucci was leaning on. Then it hit me. Sadie May must be mixed up with the Dixie mob through Bill Kent. Now that was some real bad news. I wondered if all this could have anything to do with the death of Zeebdee, and what in the world could I tell Maryjo? I headed back to the Piggly Wiggly to the cabstand there. I picked up a few more fares, not a bad day.

Later in the evening, Doris got off work. When she came out, she walked over to the car and said, "Hey, baby, how did you do today?" I told her about the fares I took in.

She lowered her eyes and said, "I'm sorry for last night."

I smiled and said, "You really went to town on that girl."

She looked at me and said, "Are you mad with me?"

I told her, "No, you didn't beat me up. I don't know about Jessie though."

She laughed and said, "Fuck Jessie, she got what she deserved. I bet that won't be the last time she will put the moves on somebody's man."

I smiled then said, "Not your man."

She looked at me for the first time and smiled. She said, "I'm glad to hear you say that. I was hoping you wouldn't think less of me for fighting like that. I don't know what got into me."

I smiled and said, "Two or three rum and cokes."

We both laughed. I told her what happened in the alley with Toy and Pap's men. She asked if I was okay.

She said, "I know you been through a lot in the Great War."

I told her yeah, but she just shook her head then.

She said, "You look tired, did you sleep okay?"

I just turned my head to keep from lying.

She said, "Please, let me know if there is anything I can do to help." She smiled and said, "I promise I'll behave myself."

I said, "Okay, on one condition." She started laughing, and I said "Give me a kiss" and she did, and that was that. I told her that I would see her soon for our date to the Smokehouse.

I went back over to Alton Park to check out the damage to Sadie May's nightclub. As I rode by, I saw the damage was complete, the club had been destroyed. I saw something else I thought was odd, it was W. B. Robinson, the so-called black police force. He was standing in the alley looking around right where Toy and I had our run-in with the Gaines boys. I wondered what in the world he was doing at the site of a burned-down nightclub. I kept going down Main Street till I got to the barbershop. I park at the off-duty part of the cabstand. When I got out of the cab, I saw Mr. Henry leaning against his cab, he was looking across the street in to the beauty parlor. I spoke to him as I passed him.

He said, "Hey, Shang, Pepsi Cola look'n for you."

I asked, "How long it been since you seen him?"

"Oh, about ten minutes ago," he said.

I said, "Thanks, I'll be in the barbershop."

I went into the shop, took a look at who was in the waiting area, and took a seat. I was hoping to talk to Robert, Tom's brother and business partner. As I waited, I heard the guys besides me talking about the fire. They talked about what they had heard. The fire had started from faulty or bad wiring, maybe something in the kitchen. Nobody was hurt, nobody was in the building at that time of the morning. *So why was W. B. Robinson snooping around the scene?* I wondered. That part kept bothering me, like when I saw Sadie May in the same place as Lenny the Lizard. I had more questions than answers. So once I got the chance to get in Robert's chair, I asked him how was Mr. Tom.

He just shook his head, he said quietly, "It don't look good."

I lower my voice and said, "It's a dam shame about the club. Man, I was there last night."

"Yeah," he said, "I don't know what could've happened all of a sudden like that."

"Yeah," I said, "it sure was out of the blue all right." I asked him, "What do you know about W. B. Robinson?"

He shook his head no but said in a whisper, "He crooked as the day is long, all he do is the Lizard's bidding. If you get in Lenny's way, he gonna be all in your face." He stopped talking quickly and took a look around. "He got spies and tattletales he pay to keep in everybody's business."

He stopped whispering and said out loud, "Man, I heard it was a big fight up on McCallie last night."

I looked surprised as I could and said, "Naw, I haven't heard nothing about that. What happened?"

"I heard Willie Green's wife caught him up in that flophouse at that corner of Dobbs. She wailed on Willie and that slick-ass Jessie that work across the street. I told Josie she gonna be trouble from the git-go. Josie always let them hot tail gals work in her shops."

I said, "Dam, you think Thelma whipped up on that Jessie?"

He said, "Willie just cut out and run once he got his ass off the ground."

I paid him and got out of the chair. As I walked away, I pulled out two more dollars and handed it to Henry to pay my cabstand rent for the week. About then, Pepsi Cola pulled up across the street. I saw Thelma get out of the car; as she did, Pepsi saw me and waved me over.

I said, "Hey, man, sorry about last night."

He shook his head then put his hand out the car window, holding $50. He said, "Naw, man, you ain't got nothing to be sorry for. Hell, you found that fool. We had him right there."

About that time, I heard a loud bang coming from the beauty shop, I saw Thelma coming back out the door, she had tears running down her face. I looked at Pepsi, he got out the car and said, "What happened?"

She just shook her head and said, "Miss Josie won't let me at her ass, she say 'Not here, got to get her away from here.'"

Pepsi handed me the money and got back in the car. Thelma looked up at me and said, "Tell Doris I said thanks, tell her we even now. She'll know what I mean. If you see Willie's ass, drag him back to my house, I need him back, we got them babies. I can't do it by myself." They pulled off then.

As the car drove away, the door to the beauty shop opened, and Josephine walked out. She strolled up to me and said, "You the man found Willie Green for Pepsi?"

I said, "Yes, ma'am, I did, but that rascal got away again."

She smiled then said, "I saw you talking to Maryjo." I nodded but said nothing, she went on. "I know she saw Big John."

I looked shocked evidently, so she said laughingly, "She my granddaughter, I know what's going on with her all day every day."

I nodded then said, "What do you want me to do? Leave it alone?"

She shook her head and said, "Hell no, you just the man for the job. I want you to find him and look into why he shot my boy." She let that last part linger, I could see the pain in her bright eyes.

She said, "Can you come by the Smokehouse tonight?"

I said, "Yeah, I'll be there."

She said "Good, see you then" and went across Main Street and got in the car as Henry held open the back door.

I wondered how she knew I talked to her granddaughter. I didn't remember seeing her and Henry around here the other day. Then it hit me, she had spies, maybe ladies in the shop or men in the barbershop. Yeah, that had to be it.

So I drove home to eat some dinner and rest up a bit. When I got home, I fed the dog. Black Jack was glad to see me. I went out to the garden and took a look at what kinda shape my crops were in. They seemed okay; I would have tomatoes soon, and my melons where coming on strong. With that done, I played with Jack and patted him up really good. Then I went in, took a shower and a nap. I woke up around 6:00 p.m. rested. No wild dreams of battles long past. I decided to shower again. It was green night, so I put on my green knit sweater to match my green slacks. I chose to wear my tan shoes with that. I grabbed a piece of corn bread to tide me over till dinner at the Smokehouse.

The food was always good there, Mr. Tom's ribs where the best in town. I drove over to pick up Doris. When she came out, I jumped out of the car to open the door for her. She looked surprised but held back from getting in the car and gave me a kiss first, it was a good kiss. I smiled, closed the door, and got in and drove toward Alton Park. The Smokehouse was on Johnson Street, it was a half a block long. The only thing back there was the Smokehouse, it was a long building that must have been some kinda store or warehouse a long time ago. Tom had added on and raised the building several times, I was told. It had been open when I was a young boy. Over the years, Tom had made it into one of the most successful businesses in town, even without the numbers.

We parked the car in the lot around the back of the building. I saw Toy's car when we parked. I had told Doris about my meeting with Miss Josie and about what had happened that afternoon. She smiled when I told her what Thelma had said. I didn't ask her what Thelma meant, so we just walked in. As we got inside, I saw Toy and Tootsie sitting at a table on the side. I walked Doris over to their table, nodded my head, and asked, "May we join you?"

Toy looked up as Tootsie, smiled, and said, "Sure." Toy nodded his head, he was a man of few words.

I guess that's why Tootsie was so eager for the company. Doris looked up at me as she sat down, and I said, "This will keep you out of trouble while I'm gone."

She giggled and said, "Let's hope Bean won't be here tonight."

About that time, I looked up, and Henry was coming toward our table. He stopped at my side of the table, spoke to everyone with a curt good evening. The ladies spoke, Toy and I nodded our heads. He looked at me and said, "Miss Josie waiting on you upstairs, top of the steps, first door on the right."

I rose from the table, as I did, I told Doris, "You know what I want."

She said, "Your ribs might not be here if you don't hurry back."

I said, "Girl, don't mess with my ribs."

When I got up the steps, the door was open. I saw Josie sitting in an office chair, holding a teacup to her lips. As I walked in, I saw Maryjo. She looked up at me then at her grandmama and looked at the floor. The room must have been some kinda office.

Josie said, "Is your last name Butler?" I nodded my head yes, then she said, "I knew your grandmother, she was a good friend of Mama Sublee. I was sorry to hear she passed away."

I looked her way and said, "Me too, I miss her every day."

"Well you seem to be a smart fellow, Mr. Butler. Am I to understand that my granddaughter hired you to look into my son's murder?"

I looked at Maryjo; as she looked up, I saw relief in her eyes, so I said, "Yes, ma'am."

"I take it she musta seen Big John?" Josie snapped, sitting her teacup down on the old desk that took up most of that side of the room.

As she did that, Maryjo sat up and said, "How do you know about that?"

Josie smiled, a clever look on her face now and spat out, "I didn't, but I do know now. So let's cut to the chase, this boy's ribs are downstairs getting cold. A cow need a bushy tail come flying time, if you don't have yours, you can borrow mine."

The funny thing was that Maryjo and I both knew what that meant. We looked at the wise-eyed old lady then at each other, and we knew that Josie meant to hire me to look into Zeebdee's killing.

I said, "Okay, you want me to find Big John then what?"

She said, "You bring him to me."

I looked at her and asked, "What about the Morton boys and Mr. Tom's bounty?"

She shook her head, and her glasses slid down her nose. She said, "Tom ain't long for this world, he got one kidney left, and he too brown to go upstairs in Erlanger Hospital so he can get hooked to a machine that could save him. We done went back and forth to the hospital so many times. We took cash money over there one time, try to give it to one doctor. He took the money then rolled Tom upstairs, put him on the dam machine. Soon as them white folk got a good look at him, they raised so much hell about a colored man being up there. We dam near had to run way from there."

She had a tear running down her face. I just shook my head. It's hard to imagine that kinda racism that would deny a man the very thing he needed to live. I said, "Sound like Tom is a condemned man."

Josie shook her head again. "I know Tom since I was twelve years old, I don't know what I'm gonna do without him."

I let that rest, then I said, "So what do I do if I can find Big John?"

She said, "If you can, bring him to me. If not, let me know where me and Henry can go to find him. If I can talk to him, I can get to the bottom of just who paid that man to shoot my boy. If you do find him, the reward money is yours. Now if you can get to the bottom of this thing and show me who the culprit is, I will pay you $5,000, but we gonna need proof."

I said, "What kinda proof?"

She said, "Any dam kind you can get."

I looked at her and then at Maryjo and said, "No matter where it goes?"

They both looked up at me then at each other. Maryjo said, "What does that mean?"

Josie looked at me and said, "Yep, that's right." Then to Mary, she said, "Child, I'll tell you later this grown folk business."

I said, "Okay, how can I get in touch?"

She said, "Henry will keep up with you. We know where you live, and you know where we be." Then she said, "Thank you, Mr. Butler."

I went back downstairs. When I got back to the table, Doris, Toy, and Tootsie were done with their meal. When I sat down, one of the waitresses came out of the kitchen with my plate of ribs, they were still hot, and my fries and onion rings were fresh.

Toy shook his head and said, "Now you done moved up in the world." He and Tootsie got up to dance when a good song started to play on the jukebox.

After I ate, I told Doris about some of the stuff that had gone on upstairs. She liked to dance, so we got up and danced a whole bunch of times. As the night drew on, we got up to leave; we told Toy and Tootsie good night. I drove home slowly, thinking about all that had happened in the last few days. I took Doris to my house, she usually stayed over on Saturday night 'cause she was off on Sunday, but she did stay over during the week sometimes too. We made love and enjoyed each other.

Before we went to sleep, she said, "Do you really think you can find Big John? If you do, what you gonna do with that killer?"

I said, "I'll cross that bridge when I come to it." She frowned at me then she fell asleep.

That morning, we a woke with the dog barking again. This time, it was the kids passing the house on their way to Warner Park. It was open early now that the weather was hot. Doris and I ate breakfast. I fed the dog, and she patted and played with him. He liked Doris. We got in the cab, and I took her home.

When we pulled up at her apartment, she frowned at me again and said, "You will be careful, won't you? I don't think I could lose another love."

I looked at her sideways and laughed. "So you love me, uh?"

She smiled then and pushed my face away as I went to kiss her. She kissed me long and hard and jumped out the cab, closed the door, turned, and said, "Let me know if I can help."

I said "Okay" then drove away.

I thought I would take a look around the neighborhood for signs of Big John. I put on my work clothes and my army boots. I walked to the end of Garfield down to Scruggs. When I got to Scruggs, there was a fence; across that fence was the train yard, least that's what we called it around here. There were trains all over the yard. There was a huge field, some trains were moving very slowly, others were just sitting, waiting to be cleaned and repaired. That's what they did in the train yard. As I walked down the fence further back into the neighborhood, the yard got bigger, then I came to a place where there was a hole in the fence. The yard had a lot of trees and overgrowth, it went on like that for about four or five blocks. I went inside the fence into the woods.

Before I left the house, I found a gun I like, a .32 caliber revolver. I had gotten it off a French soldier who was killed by machine-gun fire. I found some ammo for the gun. I noticed French officers carried .32 calliber pistols. The bullets to that gun had full metal jackets. When I fire the slugs that were in the revolver at a man on the battlefield, he barely showed signs that the bullet hit him. I was about to toss the gun in the trench when I saw a French officer fired his gun at two German soldiers; when the men got hit, they both fell down and backward. I pulled a box or two of those shells to put in my gun. So even though it fit in my pants pocket, I was still carrying heavy artillery.

As I walked into the woods, I started to think back to when I was in the Argonne Forest, fighting for my life. Soon I saw what looked like a campsite. I kept walking down the fence; as I did, I came out of the trees and saw a makeshift tent. There were two men lying on the ground, they looked at me to see if I was the police or from the railroad. When they saw that I was wearing no uniform, they sort of relaxed. I took that chance to say hello. I raised my hand in a wave. As I did, I walked toward them. They both sat up now, wondering what was I going to do next.

I said, "It's a hot day."

They said, "Yeah, it is."

Then I said, "What do you, folks, do for water around here?"

They looked at each other then back at me. Then I saw recognition in the face of the closest one to me. They were both black men, hard to say how old because all the hard living they did. Their clothes were just rags. The shoes on their feet were made of cardboard, like the ones they bury you in. They most likely found an undertaker who was kind or they may have done some digging. A lot of these men made money digging graves at the two or three graveyards here in south Chattanooga.

The man rose to his feet and said, "I know you, you live down the street. You and your grandmother have a vegetable garden."

I said, "Yeah, it's my garden now, my grandma's been gone awhile."

He shook his head then said, "Yeah, you told me. I forgot, I'm always forgetting."

I said, "My name is Shang. You been in these woods for a while?"

He nodded his head, about that time his buddy stood up. He looked at me, thought about something for a minute or two, then said, "What do you want, Shang? I'm Shep, and this Gogo. We been around here off and on for about a year now. We like the peace around these woods."

I looked at Shep and said, "I'm looking for a man, a bad man. I think he been hiding around here for quite some time. He don't travel like you, folks, he just hiding out."

He looked at Gogo then said, "You asked what we do for water? Well if you go down the fence a bit, there's a park. If you go to the edge of woods, there's a creek. It's the freshest water we can find around here." Then he said awhile back, "We went down to the creek, and we saw a man. He threw rocks at us one time, told us not to come back down there no more. We been getting water out that creek for years. Now we got to go down at night. He don't be down there late at night."

I looked in that direction and thought about what was down there. He was talking about Citico Creek, it ran around Lincoln Park on around to the city pumping station. I haven't been back in there since I was in the Tennessee Army reserve. We went down there and dug up part of the creek bed there too. That would be a place for a man like Big John to hide.

What puzzled me was why he won't be around at night. I told Shep and Gogo to come by soon and that I would have some melons and tomatoes. I told them that the weeds would be waiting. I pulled out some cash but Gogo shook his head then said, "No, you can't give us a dime. If you can get rid of that bad man down at the creek, we be happy to help."

I nodded my head then headed down the fence. Soon I saw the railroad office. I kept near the fence, hoping the men in the office didn't see me. I hugged the fence till I got to the park entrance. Lincoln Park was really a playground. There were swing sets, monkey bars, there were sandpits for playing horseshoes.

I walked to the edge of the park were there used to be a wooden fence. Now the fence was made of metal, it was taller too. I walked along the fence toward the pumping station till I got to a gate, it was closed but not locked. I went through the gate then headed down toward the creek. I could hear the water running, and the air got a bit cooler as I walked along the edge of the creek. This was the part of the creek bed that we dug up so many years ago. The work we did was still good. We dug up the choke point of the creek that would fill up with leaves and sticks then back up and flood out. Now this area was much wider, and the creek flowed well.

I walked down the other way toward the park again. After a while, the fence stopped the railroad office, and the pump house were a half a mile away. That's when I saw where Shep and his folk were able to get down to the creek. It was railroad tracks back there but not much else, no need for a fence, there was nothing to protect. If they walked around the railroad office, passed the park, you could cut through the woods and get right to the creek. I walked along the creek bank quietly. I saw that there was an old shack that was built in the late 1800s. I could smell somebody or something.

I got down low as I came up closer to the shack. When I got next to it, I looked into the old window. I saw a figure move inside the shack. I crouched down low and moved in fast, now I felt like I was back in the trenches. As soon as I got up near the front door, I pulled out the .32 caliber pistol I had in my pocket. I waited a few minutes to see if he would come out but he didn't, so I went to the door and kicked it in. When it flew open, I rushed in. I saw Big John look up, startled. I didn't wait for him to react, I put the gun in his face and told him not to move, the gig was up.

He started to get up off the stool he sat on then just flopped back down. I had seen John many times before he shot Zeebdee. He was a big, dark-skinned man with a full head of hair back then, he had a big smile, a mouth full of teeth any way. I only seen him smile once when he beat up another gambler who had accused him of cheating. Big John took pleasure pounding on the smaller man, the evil grin on his face made that real clear. Later on, we found out that

John had cheated the man. Now as I looked in the face of this brutal killer, I could see that time and rough living had taken a toll. Most of his teeth were gone; he was still tall, but the girth of the man was gone. He almost looked weak. The smell that I smelled outside the cabin was much stronger inside. John smelled so bad that I had to put my hand up over my nose and mouth to keep on talking.

I walked into the room, closed, and put my back to the door. I said, "Well, well, well, look who we have here. The killer of Zeebdee."

He shook his head no, then he started to kinda shake all over. He looked at me and said, "I know you, you the man got that garden with them good melons."

I looked shocked and said, "How you know 'bout my melons?"

John said, "You got that dog. He like them bones."

I was puzzled, I thought he was talking nonsense, then it hit me. That's why he won't be around the creek at night. He'd been roaming the alleys and parks looking for scraps, stealing out of gardens. What I thought was kids outside at night was most likely Big John.

I looked at him and said, "We got us some talking to do." He looked at me and said, "You one of Mr. Tom's men? Did you come to kill me?"

I said, "No, not if I don't have to." I moved closer so he could see the gun in my hand. I said, "Not if I don't have to." I told him that I knew someone made him shot Zeebdee and I wanted to know who and why now.

He sat up and said, "If I tell you, they gonna kill you too."

I shook my head no then said, "Who is they?"

He turned his head as if to listen. Then I heard the sound of footsteps. We both got quiet and listened as footsteps came closer to the door. When I heard someone come up to the door of the old shack, I flung the door open and ran out. As that happened, I saw a man at the door. He was so close I knocked him down as I ran by him. I looked to the right and saw two more guys, one of them raised his gun and shouted, "Reaper, I got you now." He fired his gun.

As I ran past, the bullet knocked bark off the tree near my head. As I came from behind the tree, I fired my gun three times. I heard a man holler "ouch" and then another voice say "Hold your fire, Gilbert, don't shoot."

I ran back down the hill toward the creek. I wasn't sure if they were chasing me or if they were there to get Big John. It looked like two of the men I saw in the alley behind Sadie May's, so they were Pap's men. As I ran back through the woods, a thunderstorm came up, it began to rain hard then lightning flashed. I was coming out of the woods, but the storm was getting worse, I had to find some kind of shelter.

The car was parked at the corner of Lincoln and Blackford Street. I knew enough about the neighborhood to know that the houses on that corner where that car was parked were empty. I opened the car door and got in the back seat. I was soaked down to the bone. The storm went on with thunder and lightning for a while longer. I knew that this was their car, and with all the thunder, I would not hear them coming. I only had three bullets left in my gun, not enough for a shoot-out with three of Pap's men.

As the storm died down, I climbed out of the car and headed into the big bush that was growing close to the corner near where the car was parked. I needed to know more about why John killed Zeebdee. I didn't know why Pap's men would want to hunt down Big John, but I was hoping that they wouldn't kill him. So I waited to see if they did return to the car with John in tow, or if he was still in the woods, dead or dying, I would need to go back for him, like I did so many times in the Argonne Forest in France long ago.

Shortly after I got out of the car, the rain slowed down. I heard them coming back to the car. The voice I heard first was John, he cried to them, pleading with them not to kill him or turn him over to the Morton boys. The more he cried, the louder the leader of this troop would try to reassure him that it was not the case. He kept saying "We gots to take you to see the boss. We ain't gonna kill your smelly ass." He told one of the men to put his ass in the trunk. "Pap ain't say nothing about him riding in the car." He told the man with the cast to put his ass in the trunk, "Gilbert, you may want to take your ass on round the corner to Erlanger 'cause if you still bleeding, you ain't getting in my dam car."

Now the man with the cast spoke up, he said, "Dam it, Martin, he just grazed me."

Then I heard Martin say, "I didn't hear Pap say nothing about no shoot out with no reaper, we just supposed to follow him to see if he gonna find this killer here for us."

John said, "What the hell Pap Gaines want with me?"

Then the other man spoke up, "Maybe you just a bargaining chip. We got to have something that Tom Morton want."

John tried to run and scream, but the third man took out his gun and hit him on his head. Martin turned to the third man and said, "Dam, Charlie, we could've made him get in the trunk on his own. Now y'all got to pick him up."

The man named Gilbert with the cast said, "Y'all, hell, I been shot. I'm not pick'n up no smelly ass killer."

Martin got in the car and said, "Okay, I'll just let Pap know that you, boys, won't up for the job."

The two men grabbed John and put him in the trunk as Martin got out to open it up. I heard all this while in the bushes near the car. When they finally pulled away, I came out and went home. After I showered, I fixed myself some more of the greens and corn bread. As I ate, I thought about what Pap's men had said. They were following me. I had led them straight to the killer. I wondered how they knew I was looking for Big John. Why did they not know we were in the shack if they had been following me? I considered what the man named Charlie said, John was to be a bargaining chip, but for what?

I had to talk to somebody, so I came out in my back-yard and did a bit of work in my garden; the rain had done my melons good. The vines were all green and stiff looking. After I fed the dog, I pulled some weeds. As evening rolled around, I saw what I was hoping to see. Maryjo was walking to the store. I called her from in front of my house. She saw me and waved.

She came back out of the store with her bags. She said, "Hey, Mr. Shang, how are you?"

"Hey," I said. "I'm well, but we have a problem."

I told her about my afternoon. She looked kinda scared when I told her about all the shooting, I asked her, "Why do you think Pap's men would need John as a bargaining chip?"

She thought a while then said, "I know why, maybe. They think I don't know much, but I know what's going on with Mr. Tom's business. Pap's men want to run the numbers for Mr. Tom. They can't sell no numbers in St. Elmo 'cause Mr. Tom's numbers come out earlier than the ones that Bill Kent and Lenny's game."

When she said that, I looked at her to see if she knew about her mom and the Glenwood numbers man. She didn't show any signs of recognition. So I moved on. "Do you think they'll keep him alive?" I said.

"I think they will if they want Mr. Tom to let them in his numbers game. If they keep him alive, they got something might make Tom say yeah," she said.

I looked at her then with a bit of admiration, the young lady did know a bit about the business. Then I said, "I need to tell Miss Josie what went on here. I don't want this to be no surprise."

She nodded her head and said, "I'll call her soon as I get home."

I said, "Tell her to call me, I'll be here waiting. I need to know how she want to proceed here. Looks like somebody gonna have to deal with Pap one way or another."

Later that evening, my phone rang, it was Doris, calling to see if I had made it back out of them woods. I told her what happened. She wanted me to come pick her up so she could see about me. I told her that I was tired, that we could get together tomorrow. I was relieved when she said okay. I was afraid that I would have one of those dam dreams while she was here and I would scare her to death or worse. After that call, I went and sat on my back porch where I could hear the baseball game. The lights and the noise from the park would light up the whole neighborhood. The home team was losing tonight, but I didn't care. All I had on my mind was what to do about Big John.

Next thing I knew, I was asleep again. When I woke up, the phone was ringing. I grabbed it and said hello. It was Mr. Henry, he said, "Hey, Shang, Miss Josie want to talk to you, but right now we up here at the dam hospital. Tom don't look good, he was unconscious when she found him this evening."

I asked if they were still in the basement. He said, "Yeah, we still stuck down here."

I told him that I would be by shortly. When I hung up, I showered and put on my gray pants and my gray shoes. I found my yellow knit shirt. I started to walk then thought better of it. There was no telling what my next move was, so I took the cab and my big gun .45 caliber service revolver. I also reloaded the .32 pistol that I had fired earlier. I put a hawkbill knife in my sock, just in case all else fails.

I went by the hospital and parked in the colored section, which was in the back, where the door to the colored section was. When I walked in the door of the basement area of Erlanger Hospital, all you could see was the pipes and stuff. You got to walk all the way around toward the front of the hospital where the colored nurses' station was, then you got to tell somebody who you there for. That always depends on how busy they were at the time. I found a lady behind the counter, told her who I wanted, and she pointed me in the right direction. When I walked in the colored intensive care area, it was clear that things weren't going well. They had some tubes running from all kinds of places in Tom's body, he looked like he was all puffed up with fluid.

I turned my head then because I had seen too many people die in hospitals and on the battlefields and in trenches. They may call me the reaper, but when it came to death, we were not good friends. Hell, he took my grandmother, she was eighty-seven, but I still needed her. Now looked like it was Mr. Tom's turn. I walked down the hall to where there was a makeshift waiting area. There were no seats, just crates and hard boxes where colored folk could wait to see what the outcome would be. I saw Miss Josie sitting on a hard box and Henry standing near her. She waved me over.

She said, "Maryjo told me all I need to know. I'm gonna need you to handle this for me, but first we got to see 'bout my Tom." She shook her head and said sadly, "Did you see him? He don't look good not good at all."

I asked her what happened. She looked down at the floor and said, "When I came in this evening to bring him his dinner, he was just lying there on the floor. Me and Henry brought him down here again." She stopped talking as tears rolled down her face. She said, "The dam machine upstairs, but he too brown. They won't let him go back up there."

All I could do was shake my head. A black man can go across the world to fight in wars, but here in the land of the free and the home of the brave, they can't go upstairs to use a lifesaving machine. It should be a crime the way they have treated my people. Soon after that, a young white man came around the corner, he hung his head a bit when he saw us. When he walked up to us, I could see a tear in his eye. He told us that Tom was gone.

He said that he tried. "I did everything I could."

I knew then that he must have been the one who took Tom upstairs. He looked so sad. After a few minutes, he just walked away, saying he was sorry and just shaking his head.

When he left, Josie looked up and down the hall. She said, "Henry, go in there and cover Tom up."

Henry said, "What?"

She said, "You heard me, cover him up and don't let no dam looky loos near that dam bed."

Henry said, "Okay." He left and went around the corner to do what she said.

She turned to me and said, "We got to get him out of here, Shang. Go get that hearse, bring it to that big door in back where we parked."

I looked at her, shocked at first. Then I got it. She didn't want the word out that Tom was gone. I said, "I pick him up then what?"

She said, "We got a Morton funeral parlor down in Rossville. I'll call him now. You get moving, boy. Times a wasting."

I left, went right back down the street, and got the hearse. When I pulled up, the young doctor was standing in front of the big door. He tapped on the door, and it opened.

Henry and Josie were pushing a gurney. As I got out, opened up the door, Josie told Henry to get the car. Me and Josie rolled the dolly into the back of the car and closed the door.

As we did, she turned to the doctor and said, "How much we owe y'all for all this?"

He looked at her with a sad grin and said, "For what, letting him die?" He turned his head, but I could see that he was crying again.

By that time, Henry was ready with the car. She told me to follow them to Rossville. When we got there, two men were standing near the entry door to the back of the funeral parlor. We dropped Tom off there. Then we stopped on McFarland Street at the Stateline Diner.

Josie said, "We got to get a plan right now. We can bury Tom down New Orleans' way. When I talked to Mattie Lee tomorrow, I'll make all the arrangements." She said, "Now, Shang, I need you to drive Tom down there so won't nobody know he gone. Men like Pap ain't gonna make no deal with me. As long as we keep Tom alive in his head and everyone else's, we can make some kinda deal to keep the peace and still keep this thing afloat. We got too much going here with Maryjo in school and all them folks we got working for us. All them Morton boys and their families, I need to find out who behind the killing of my boy 'cause if he were here now, I wouldn't have to worry 'bout all this mess."

I agreed to take Tom's body to New Orleans. I told her that I would be ready to leave as soon as tomorrow. She said, "If not, the next day."

My biggest problem was Doris. I was supposed to pick her up the next day. If I told her, she may let the cat out of the bag. So I came up with a cover story. When she got in the car, we went by the diner on Dobbs that she liked. After we ate, she wanted to go to my house to make sure that everything was okay. We went out in my backyard and sat awhile. There was no ball game that night, so it was really quiet. We made love, then we slept, or at least she did. I laid awake most of the night, I had too much on my mind.

After a while, I fell asleep, and one of those dreams was waiting for me. This time, it was just me in the Argonne Forest, walking alone like I did a few days ago, then out of the blue came the sound of thunder then rain. I kept walking, soon I saw them, they were waiting, some standing, some lying down, but it was a field full of killers, Pap's men, Big John, and a bunch of men from WW1. They were bleeding and crying out for help. I guess I must have cried out myself. When I woke up, Doris was sitting on the side of the bed, looking at me. I looked at her. When I did, she said nothing, she just hugged me and kissed me. We made love and held each other till we both fell asleep again.

When we woke up, it was daylight. I told Doris my cover story, that I had to go out of town for a funeral. She seemed okay with that, at least I would be out of reach of Pap's men for a while. I took her home after we stopped off on a couple of errands. When she got out of the car, she turned to face me and said, "You know I'll be here when you get back. Come by soon as you get back to town, and I can tell you what's been going on around here."

I said, "Okay."

When I got home, I put my bags in the hearse and was ready to roll. That night, I got the call. I was to pick up Mr. Tom's remains at midnight. Then looked to be in New Orleans twelve hours later. Not much happened during the trip, and the funeral was just as uneventful. Josie, Mary,

Henry, and Robert where the only people there that I knew. Mattie Lee, Bobby Ganno, and his son, Eric, and some of his men where there too. They introduced them at the repass.

The family had caught the train to town, and as soon as it was over, they were all back on the train, but they told me to stay the night and rest up. I would drive back in the morning. After I put the family back on the train, I was to return to the Ganno Mansion. When I arrived, Mattie Lee was waiting for me. They put me up in the guesthouse in the back of the mansion. When she brought my dinner out or had it brought out, she came in to tell me the plan. When I left in the morning, I was to have company, three men would ride back to town with me. I was to drop them off at the funeral home in Rossville. They were black men that looked white.

Bobby Ganno's son, Eric, who I was told was very fond of Tom, on the ride back told me more about the plan. He told me that he and his men would now help me look into finding out who killed Zeebdee and then do whatever was needed to be done about it. I was to continue to do my investigation, and they would provide whatever backup I needed. Not the Morton boys or the Sublees. They would be around when I needed them, but they would stay out of sight as long as possible. One of the men was called Chi Chi, he had white skin, but his hair was not like a white man's. The other was a man named Luke, his skin was white, but his nose and lips were not. Eric, too, looked the part of a white man, his hair, face, and skin were right, but his eyes gave him away, they were brown and showed too much feeling.

When I got them dropped off, I went home, showered, ate, then I called Doris. She was ready to get together. When

I drove up and looked in the window, she was already up front. She waved and came out the front door of the store. She got in the car and gave me a kiss. She asked how I was then started asking question almost nonstop. I finally got a few words in to ask if anybody heard anything about Big John.

She said, "No, but people still saying Willie Green got money."

I told her that he was no longer my concern. We decided that we would go by Pauline's in St. Elmo the next night. She knew I was tired, so she let me go home.

I drove by the cabstand and told Henry who was standing next to the shoeshine stand that things were going as planned. As I got out of the cab, I saw the blue Chevy that Willie Green was driving, it was parked on Main Street with a for sale sign in the window. I smiled when I saw Pepsi Cola sitting in his car down the street. I ran a few fares just as we planned it. We knew that we were being watched, all of us at some point or another. When I went home that night, there was a ball game. I sat on my back porch and listened to the game, this time the lookouts were winning. I ate a bowl of greens and corn bread. When the game was over, I went to bed. I slept well, so I was up early working in the garden.

I looked up when Black Jack started to bark and saw Shep and Gogo coming down the alley. They stopped by the gate, and I let them in the backyard after I tied up Black Jack. We spoke our hellos then got down to work. They had weeded the beds many times, so they knew the ropes. Then we got down to picking vegetables. When that was done, I told them that the woods behind Lincoln Park should be clear. They thanked me and headed out. I showered and started to get dressed. We said it was gray night, I put on my gray plaid slacks with my white-and-gray shirt that I had made by Miss Moody, then I put on my slate gray sport coat and my gray shoes. When I got to the store, Doris was waiting out front, she had on a light gray dress with pearl gray heels on. She looked good in gray. When we got to Pauline's, which was on Glenlyn Road, I noticed the car I had seen Pap's men were driving, which meant that at least one of the men that took Big John away was here.

We ate our food and got up and danced a few times to the music that played on the jukebox. When we got ready to go, we walked out to the car. I noticed two men that I had never seen before coming up behind us. I had put what I called my big, little gun in my belt in back of me. I put the .32 in my jacket pocket. I put my hand on the gun in my back. I told Doris to move between the cars when I told her to. She promised me that she would do as I said if there was trouble on this date, so soon as I told her, she moved over away from me and the two men at the back of us. About that time, three more men came out from behind the cars up ahead. One of them had a cast on his hand. He was my new enemy. He smiled when he saw me reach in my jacket and pulled out the Luger.

He said, "Dam, I ain't seen one of them in a long time. Does that thing still shoot?"

I said, "Yeah, we gonna sure find out."

He pointed to the men at the back of me, and they had their guns drawn too. The guys beside him drew their guns too. When I looked over at Doris, she had her hand in her purse. One of the guys at the back of us pointed his gun her way.

The man with the cast started to speak, he said, "We the Stevens boys. I had heard you was a brave man, but you was a dam fool to bring this woman."

Doris sneered. "I can take care of myself."

Right at that moment, car lights came on, they were bright. A man came out from behind that car, he said, "Hold on just a minute here, Gill."

When I could finally see who it was, Bean Gaines was standing between me and the three men in front of me. Bean turned to me and said, "I don't think you gonna need that German cannon tonight."

I put the gun down to my side and put my hand out for Doris to join me. She came out from between the cars and stood by me. Bean smiled his gold-fronted grin and said, "Hello, there, Doris."

She fought back a smile as she waved her hand.

Then Gill, the man with the cast, said, "Dam it, Bean, we got unfinished business here. Me and this man got us a score to settle."

Bean turned his head, and Charlie and Martin came out from the car that I saw earlier. Bean's smile faded a little when Martin spoke up, he said, "Gilbert, you started this shit. When we went in that alley, we was just supposed to talk to Toy. You knew better than to call Shang the reaper."

Gill said, "Well, now we got a score to settle 'cause he broke my dam wrist."

Bean shook his head and said, "Enough of this crap, Gill. You, boys, need to fall back now, we got things to work out here. This fellow Shang is a very important man. Hell, he the man found Big John."

Right then, I saw Eric, Chi Chi, and Luke, who was holding a bar rifle (Browning Automatic Rifle), coming from behind another car. Bean's smile disappeared, he snapped his head around and put his hands up. He said, "Well, now who do we have here? These ain't no Morton boys."

Eric smiled then walked into the light. As soon as Gill saw Luke with the bar, he began to back away from the circle, he and the rest of the Stevens boys turned to leave. Martin and Charlie leaned on their car.

Bean put his hands down and stepped toward Eric, and he said, "Looks like we got some new players in this game." He put out his hand and told Eric his name, and in an introduction way, I said, "This is Eric."

I did not say Ganno because the plan was to keep that part under wraps until we could get more info about Zeebdee's real killer.

Eric said, "Can we get down to brass tacks here?"

Bean shook his head yes then said, "Pap gonna love you. We got that killer on ice. All we needs to do is come to some kinda agreement about that numbers game Tom and them gots."

Eric turned his head to look around the lot then said, "Yes, we can. I want to meet Pap, is he your brother?"

Bean shook his head said, "No, we cousins. We got a big deal going from here on down through Georgia. My game is gals, but Pap's got the numbers thing working."

Eric said, "We need to get together on this now or as soon as possible."

Bean said, "You and Shang can come by tomorrow, we can meet up on Lafayette Road at the Stateline diner. Then we can take a little ride down the country."

We agreed then all got in our cars and left. As I pulled out, I noticed a familiar car in the lot near the exit. It was Bill Kent's car. I told Doris that this would have to be the end of her part in this adventure. She turned her head and looked out the window. "Lookout Mountain is always pretty at night," she said. "I won't scared. I knew you were there."

She and I went back to my house and made love. I dropped her off at her apartment that morning and went to meet Eric at the Rossville funeral parlor where I had dropped them off. He was leaning on the blue Chevy that belong to Willie Green. He smiled when he saw me checking out the car. I told him about Willie's windfall.

Eric shook his head and said, "One man's trash is another man's gold." He tossed me the keys then said, "I hope you know where we're going."

I nodded my head and said, "We will find out soon enough."

When we pulled up in the diner lot, it was around 8:30 a.m. Charlie was standing in front of his car waiting. I pulled up in a parking spot next to his car. We said our good mornings, then Eric asked where Bean was.

Charlie smiled and said, "Bean don't get up this early. He went down there last night when we left the club." He asked had I ever been to Lafayette. When I said yeah, he said, "good, so you won't get lost." He laughed then pulled out.

We headed down Lafayette Road right away, it turned to US Route 27. After about ten miles, we slowed down as we passed through the small town of Noble, Georgia. We pulled in to the town of Lafayette around nine thirty. We stopped off at one house then the other to let folks know that we were here, then we pulled up in front of our destination, Pap's house. It was a big house, had to have a least four bedrooms upstairs and maybe a few in the back. As we started to get out of the car, the front door opened, the man on the porch was Pap Gaines.

He smiled when he saw us come up on the porch, and said, "Good morning, gentlemen, I'm Pap Gaines."

We both gave our names and shook his hand. Then we got down to business. I waited on the front porch with Charlie as Eric and Pap went around the yard looking at Pap's wife's garden and talking business. After a while, two young men came out on to the porch. Charlie said, "These were Pap's nephews, James Theodore, and his brother, Bethel."

They were both almost grown men, had to be eighteen or so. They had BB guns. They began to put on a show; James Theodore seemed real interested in the Morton's while he and his brother shot at birds, flies, bees, and anything else they could find. Their aim was amazing, they didn't miss much. James finally asked me if I had seen Maryjo. I told him that I had seen her. That brought a bout of laughter from his brother, Bethel. Soon a full-blown BB gun battle broke out, and the boys shot each other with the BB guns until I looked up and Bean was standing on the porch. He gave the boys one look, and they stopped. Bean then told me that James Theodore was going into the Army reserve so he could go to school on that new G.I. Bill. Bean told the boys to go on up the road to get the rest of their cousins. "We gonna have lunch soon."

When they were gone, Bean said, "That boy gonna be something one day." He and Charlie told me how James's and Bethel's daddy was killed in a knife fight when the boys were young, and without a daddy, the boys were wild as hell. About that time, Pap and Eric came back up on the porch.

Eric looked pleased. He said, "It would be a good thing for the Mortons and the Gaines to join up."

Bean smiled and said, "We gonna have to talk about this thing with the Stevens boys and this man right here," and he put his hand on my shoulder.

Pap looked at Charlie and said, "I been told there was some bad blood. What can we do to settle this thing up? I understand there was a gun pulled on a woman."

I raised my eyebrow at Pap as he shook his head with disapproval, then he said, "That dam Gilbert has never learned to keep his mouth shut."

Eric looked at me to see what I may say. I looked at Pap and Bean and said, "I'll let it go if they will."

The Gaines boys looked at each other then at me, and Pap said, "I heard you was a brave man and easygoing too." I smiled and looked away.

After that, more men came, it was the Marsh boys, most of whom had driven down from noble. After lunch, which was delicious by the way Pap's wife, Ginny Lou, was a hell of a cook, we all got in the cars and drove north. When we got to Noble, the Marsh boys drove around to the edge of a farm that was off the main drag. As we drove into the farmyard, we got out of the cars and had to walk further into

the farmyard. There was a small barn in the back of the prop-
erty near the woods. Me, Pap, Eric, and Bean followed one
of the Marsh boys who owned the place. We walked to the
back where they had Big John fastened down in a small barn.
As we started to brace the killer, he wouldn't talk till they let
him come out of the barn. When he came out, I pulled out
my gun. Pap and Bean went back up the trail a few feet away.
Eric pulled out a small tape recorder, then he began to ask the
killer all the right questions. From what I heard, it was Bill
Kent who had the leverage on the killer after W. B. Robinson
locked him up. His mother had put up her house for bail. He
spoke slow. I heard a sound in the woods; when I looked, I
saw the muzzle flash then heard the shot. As I ducked down,
I saw Big John fall back.

When I looked up with my gun in hand, I saw that Eric
was exposed. I took aim and fired the Luger in the direction of the muzzle flash, then I heard two more shots. As I
looked around, the Gaines boys were pinned down on the
yard. I could hear the Marsh men running in our direction.
About this time, I looked in the woods again, there was more
than one shooter now. Pap started to fire his gun, he saw the
men in the woods too. He fired, he'd hit one every time he
fired, one would drop or holler. Eric was pinned down with
no cover between the woods and the barn. I told him to get
down low, use the body for cover as Jon and I had done years
ago. He hesitated at first, then as the shots came in closer, he
got behind the body. There seemed to be one man aiming at
the boy, so I took the Luger and aimed it a little high, it had
at least nine shots left. I knew that if I fired it in rapid fire as

I had seen German officers do, it would send all the bullets in a tight pattern.

As I fired all the rounds, I could see that I was right. As the gun emptied, it sent all the rounds at the man who was shooting at Eric. I thought I heard him yell out, then I got up to move. I was hoping to pull Eric out of that spot he was in, but as I rose, I drew the fire of the man that was shooting at him. He fired high at first when I felt the shot go just over my head. I took the .32 that I had in my pocket and shot that at the same spot I did before, this time I heard nothing, then two more shots from him lower this time, but my little cover saved me. I turned to look, it was a bush hog and an old tractor. I kept going; as I did, I shouted to Eric to stay down and that I'll be back. I headed for the Chevy; I knew we had the bar rifle in the trunk. As I turned the corner, I saw that there were men running all over the farmyard shooting. Some were Marsh boys, some weren't. Every now and then, the ones that weren't would shoot at me too. After a few more close calls, I got to the Chevy, opened up the trunk, and pulled out the bar. I saw Pap and Bean standing behind the car, they came in as they took out their long guns. I knew that things were about to change. I turned and cocked the gun.

When Pap saw that gun, he grabbed Bean and said, "Hold up, let him get ahead of us with that broom." Then Pap yelled, "Sweep it clean. Shang!"

I fired the gun at a few men. I could see that they weren't the Marsh boys. As I got back near the woods, I could hear Pap and Bean cleaning up behind me. I waited till he fired on Eric again, then I took the bar and went to work. The gun was a rapid fire 30.06 caliber, that's a big bullet made to push through brush or any kind of cover. As soon as I started firing, the sniper in the woods was running the first few rounds I fired. I heard him holler then he rolled away. As soon as I heard that, I lowered the gun and moved up to Eric's position, the boy was wild-eyed by now. When I went to move him, he pushed me away at first, like he couldn't see me at all. I've had many soldiers react the same way, so I knew what to do. I called him by his name calmly, then as he came around, I put my hand out. As he took my hand, I saw that he was bleeding in two or three places, looked like he had been grazed more than one time. I got him to his feet, we were ready to run. At first, the boy was wobbly, then as I picked up the gun, he got his feet under him. He stopped then looked down at his side, the recorder was dirty but still intact. When we got to the car, Pap and Bean were waiting, they were both glad to see that the boy was okay.

They confirmed that it was Bill Kent's men that made the attack, this meant that Bill Kent knew about the merging between the Gaines and Mortons. We got in the car after we got out the farm's first aid kit. I knew enough that I could wrap up the two bullet burns that were on his arm and shoulder. When we got in the car, Eric told Pap that he would be in touch. As we rode back home, the boy was quiet at first, then he said, "I forgot to say thank you. You saved my life back there. I knew you would come back for me. I'm told you were in the Great War, that you saved many men on the battlefield, is that true?" He looked at me.

When I didn't say anything, he said, "How did you know?"

"Know what?" I asked.

"That I could use that man's body to cover myself?"

I told him that I had seen it done before. He looked at me and said, "Thank you for sharing that with me, I'll never forget it."

When I dropped him off at the funeral home, Chi Chi and Luke were sitting in the back, smoking something that didn't smell like a cigarette. When they saw the boy, they jumped to their feet to see about him. They were both beside themselves. I think it was the fact that they would have to answer to Bobby Ganno if the boy was to come to harm.

He and I gave them the short version of what happened, then I got in the cab and drove home. I made sure that nobody was following me. Looked like I was gonna have to work on that. This must be the third or fourth time that I been followed and ambushed. I called Doris to let her know that I was back. We talked a while, but I didn't let her know about the day's excitement. We made a plan to get together the next night, she picked red this time, so that meant I would wear something red. After I ate a bowl of honeydew and watermelon, I showered then called the number that Eric gave me. When he answered, I told him about my theory that Bill Kent's men were a distraction, they were there to cover up the real shooter's tracks. And that I was almost sure it had to be Max Lucci.

Eric listened then said, "After a bit of thought, we need to prove Lenny and Max are involved. Then we can have them taken care of."

I told him what I had seen while I was in Glenwood: that meeting with Sadie May, Kent, and Lenny; how it looked when Sadie came out and walked away, and the fact that it was the same day as the fire, it all had to mean something. Eric told me to meet him at Josie's house, that he would send a car around for me in the morning. He agreed that we were for sure being followed around. Now we had to make a new plan.

I woke up to a knock on my door, it was Henry. He told me to take the cab to the cabstand and park it then walk into Robert's barbershop and that there would be a car at the back for me to drive. He gave me the keys then. When he left, I showered and shaved, grabbed myself a bowl of cantaloupes, and headed out in the cab. When I got behind the barbershop, I found a tan Ford; I started it up and found a note that told me where to pick up Eric. When he got in the car, he told me that he and Miss Josie were going to confront Sadie May. She and Maryjo were at the beauty parlor on Central Avenue that Josie owned. He said that she and Maryjo got their hair done there every week or so. We pulled in around the back of the shop. We sat in the parking lot a few minutes till a car pulled up and Josie got out and went in, followed by Mr. Henry. Soon the ladies in the shop all came outside.

That was our cue to go in. When we got to the door, Henry was there, he told us to hold back and listen. There was a lot of yelling and screaming at first, most of it coming from Sadie May. She kept saying that she had no idea who killed Zeebdee. She stopped yelling when Maryjo yelled, "It was Bill Kent, that's who's behind it."

Sadie May got quiet then, and Josie said, "We got proof if you will just listen."

She played the tape, we could hear the killer's voice, heard him telling his story before the shot rang out that took his life. Then it got quiet again. We heard Sadie may start to cry, she wept and spoke at the same time, she didn't want to own any nightclub, she wanted to be a schoolteacher. She said, "I went to college, you know." She said that Tom and Zeebdee got her involved in the Smokehouse at first, keeping the books and managing the supplies. "Next thing I know, Tom went and got me a club."

She told Zeebdee that she wanted out of the club and the numbers racket. She said that she and Zeebdee had a big fight about a week or two before he was killed. She said that Zeebdee lost his temper and slapped her. He knew then that he had made a big mistake. Knowing her temper, he took a step back, and she had time to pull out her gun. He was gone before she could fire it, but he knew that he would have to stay away from her until she could cool off. So he didn't come home. She said that Bill Kent was always around, trying to talk to her, telling her all about all the big real estate deals he had going on. Soon she got the idea to get out of the club business with Tom being sick and Zeebdee gone. She could burn down the club and collect the insurance money.

I heard Josie speak, asking her how she burned down the club. Sadie said that Pay had left town on a plane then drove back in town and set the club on fire that night. Josie asked her about her meeting with Kent and Lenny the Lizard, the white mob boss. Then Sadie May started to cry again, she said that Kent lied to her. He told her that she would get all the money from the club so she could buy a nice apartment building, but it turned out that the insurance company was owned by Lenny or he had his hooks in it.

"He took half of the money, but they gave me a deal on a building in Eastdale."

They told her that if she didn't go for the deal, they would have W. B. Robinson, their crooked colored cop, to look into who set the fire, that would mean Pay may go to jail for helping her get out of the club business. Josie told Henry to bring us in.

When we walked in, Maryjo looked up at me and started to speak, but Josie put up her hand and said, "We gonna need you to help us get Bill Kent."

Sadie May nodded her head. She told Maryjo to go outside. When she left, we got together a plan: she would call for a meet or date with Kent then get him to talk. We would send her in with the tape recorder so we could get the whole thing on tape. After that, Josie agreed to let Sadie May out of the club and numbers business. Now we just needed to find out when the meet would be so we could be nearby and we could control the outcome.

I took Eric back to the barbershop and picked up another car. Eric drove off in the Ford, I had a Dodge waiting for me in the alley. While we were riding, Eric told me that he had Pap's men pick up cars down in Lafayette. They would be picking them up and dropping off cars for us all over town.

I went home and got ready for my date with Doris. It was red night, so I put on my red-and-black knit shirt and my black pants and shoes. When I got to the store, she was waiting on the back side of the lot where we had agreed to meet, knowing that we were being watched. When she got in the car, she seemed distracted, so I asked her what was on her mind. At first she was quiet, then I could see that she didn't want to tell me what it was.

She just said, "Nothing, it was no big deal."

So I knew then I was gonna have to wait, she would tell me when she was ready.

We went back to Pauline's because we knew that was one place we would not be watched. Pap's men were checking every car in the lot. We got a good table and ordered drinks. The band that was playing was nice, so we got up to dance a few times after we ate. As we sat and talked, I could see that she was still carrying something around, so I asked again what had happened.

She looked around and said, "Let's get ready to go, I'll tell you on the way home."

When we got in the car, she said, "I know you gonna think I brought this on myself." Then she looked out the window at the incline again and told me what had happened. Jessie, her sister, and two cousins came by the store. They told Doris that they were going to get her for what she had done to Jessie that night in front of the flophouse. She said that Simon was ready to call the police. She was able to talk him out of it after they left. They made a big scene and tore up some of the merchandise. She told Simon that she would pay for the stuff, it was about ten dollars. They told her that they would be back every day till the score was settled.

I was silent for a beat too long, so she said, "I hope you won't turn your back on me now, I may need your help."

I spoke up and said, "You know you can count on me no matter what. I will be there in your corner."

She smiled then and said, "I'm not scared of them. If I could take them on one at the time, I would gladly face them any day, but all four of them would be too much. Even if I use my blade, I don't think I could hold them off."

"Well," I said, "I have lots of guns, if it was to come to that."

She turned her head and looked my way, maybe just to see if I meant what I said. When we got to the house, I showed her my gun shelf. She took a look at all the small guns I had. She picked up a small .32 caliber pistol I had with an inner hammer. The gun came from the trenches of the Great War, but it would still do the job. I told her that she was welcomed to take the gun and carry it around with her if that would make her feel safer. I didn't know what else I could do at the moment, so I left it at that. I would have to look into this some more before I could help her solve this problem.

We talked a while, then we both fell asleep side by side on the bed. I found myself walking in the woods again, it was still and quiet. As I walked, I could see that there was a storm coming way out on the edge of the forest, the sky was black. And I could see lightning flashing. As I looked around me, I could see men sitting and standing near a big lake. As I turned my head, lightning struck the water, and it begin to burn. The fire was bright and hot, I put up my arm to shield myself from the flames. About that time, I could hear Doris calling me. When I opened my eyes, she was there. She had a wet rag and was wiping my face and chest down with it. She put the rag down and kissed me. She was in tears, and I could feel her tremble in my arms. I just held her and let her cry it out. When she was done, she and I both fell asleep.

We both awakened with a start to the sound of the phone ringing. I grabbed it and said hello. It was Eric. He said, "Sorry to wake you. We have a meet set up. I'll meet you at the Smokehouse at twelve noon, if that will be okay."

I asked him what time was it now, he said it was 9:00 a.m. I told him that I would be there. The way we had things set up, I would drop Doris off and pick up a car in the lot at the Piggly Wiggly. That would get whatever tail I had on me from my house off me. Doris put the gun in her purse. I asked her if she knew how to use the gun.

She shook her head and said, "Yeah, my daddy taught me how to use a gun when I started dating men."

I smiled at the thought of a man, a father hoping to keep his daughter safe. When I dropped her off, I found the other car in the lot where it was supposed to be. Another Ford, a green one this time. I rode by the cabstand and saw that my cab had been moved, it was parked in the back lot behind Robert's barbershop. I passed by there on my way to the Smokehouse.

When I got there and parked around the back, I saw Eric and his men sitting and standing next to a Hudson. Luke was behind the wheel. Chi Chi was closing down the trunk. Eric got up from the passenger seat, walked over to my car to tell me the plan. Sadie May was to meet up with Bill Kent tonight. I had told them about the privacy and seclusion of Lincoln Park, so we told Sadie May, who was very familiar with the area because she played there as a child. She wondered at first if she could get Kent to drive back there, but after a bit of thought, she said, "I'll get him back there."

Eric and I would be hiding behind that big bush I had used before. Luke and Chi Chi would stay near the entrance of the park to make sure that none of Kent's men didn't try an attack of some kind. This would give us some control of the situation. When the time came, we would be ready to deal with Kent if he tried to hurt Sadie May.

Little did we know that when she got in the car, Sadie May pulled out her pistol and told Kent to drive around the corner from the Sublee home over into Lincoln Park. When the car pulled to the curb, we sat near the big bush I had used earlier to spy on Pap's men when they took Big John away. As the car pulled up, I could hear Sadie May shout, "Now you gonna tell me the truth."

When Kent started to say something, I heard a cracking sound, and Kent let out a yelp of pain. Then it got quiet, Kent started talking; he said, "Yes, I knew why Zeebdee was killed, he was going to be in the way. For years, Lenny the Lizard was plotting to take over the numbers game in Chattanooga. Tom was not gonna let them in on his game, not as long as he was alive. So knowing that, Lenny figured that if Zeebdee was gone, there would be no one left to stand in his way."

As soon as he stopped talking, I heard Sadie May say, "What was your part in this? I know you played a role in this, tell me what you did." She raised the gun up in his face.

When he didn't speak right away, she took the gun back and hit him again, this time harder because he yelled out in pain. Then as he started to cry, I heard him say, "Yeah, I set him up. I had this woman flirt with him, get his nose open. She told him to meet her at the bar in Avondale. I got him there, but Lenny was the one put Big John up to it, not me, it was Max gave him the gun. Then they told W. B. Robinson to let him go after he did the deed."

When he said that, I heard Sadie scream, She raised the gun up and hit him two or three times before we could get around the big bush to open up the car door. By this time, Sadie had made a mess of Kent's face.

I opened up the car door and grabbed her by the arm. As I did that, she came out of the car with the gun, still pointed at Kent. I could see that she was about to shoot him, so I grabbed her arm, which turned the barrel a bit so the shot she fired went out the back window of Kent's Caddie. As I pulled her back from the car, Eric came up behind me to get the tape recorder. When I let her arm go, I could see why they called her Hurricane Sadie. She took her free hand and pushed me out of the way and went to take aim at Kent again. By this time, Chi Chi and Luke had come around the bush. I thought that the shot she fired must have clued them that it was time to close the show. Luke grab her and lifted her up, raising her gun hand again. She started to fight, but I was able to calm her down. I spoke softly to her and told her that she was done, out of the club and numbers racket. All she had to do was walk away, let it go, and walk away now.

I heard her say, "Okay, okay. Just take your hands off me, just let me be."

As we backed away from her, she put the gun down to her side. I could see tears running down her face. She was a proud woman, and she had been used and fooled into taking part in the murder of her husband. Now the plan was for me to drive her back to the Sublee house in one of the cars that we drove to the park. Luke, Chi Chi, and Eric would take care of Kent. I was not told what they had planned for him.

Earlier that evening, I had showed the men where I had found Big John. We walked all over the woods down and around Citico Creek. They took a good look at the creek bed and how wide and deep the water got as the creek fed into the Tennessee River, lots of fast-moving currents and deep water.

I got Sadie May in the car and drove out of the park. She had quit crying but was real quiet I asked if she was okay. She looked out the window of the car and said, "I used to love Lincoln Park when I was a little girl. I don't think I will ever go out there again."

She looked at me, then as we pulled up in front of her mother's house, she said, "Thank you. Mr. Shang, thank you so much." She put her purse on her arm and got out of the car.

I was almost sure that she was thanking me for keeping her from becoming a murderer. It's one thing to make money writing numbers or running a nightclub, but killing is a whole other matter. Cold blood is not so easy to wash off your soul. I know 'cause of those dreams I have.

Now my part of this was over for the moment. When I got home, I called Doris to get the report of how her day went. When she picked up the line and we said our hellos, she told me that the ladies came back by the store, this time Simon was there to keep them from damaging the store. A white man threatening to call the cops was a good deterrent. This time it was only two of them. I told her to hang in there, it just might get back down to just Jessie, and we both know that she could handle her. She laughed at that, it was good to hear her laugh. I talked to her a while, then we set up a date to go to the Ball Park. We had started going to the games when the weather got warm. We would walk over from my house, eat dinner at the park, the hot dogs and fries were good with soda or beer.

When I hung up from her, I went out in the backyard and fed the dog, he liked to eat at night. I sat out on the back porch till I heard the phone ring. When I picked up, it was Henry on the line. He told me to meet him and Josie at the Smokehouse at noon so we could settle up. I thanked him and said that I would be there.

That morning before I went to the Smokehouse, I stopped by the barbershop and picked up the cab, it was still in the lot behind Robert's barbershop. I left the Ford in the lot. I would give the keys to Henry when I got to the Smokehouse. It was a good morning to work the cabstand, so I drove the cab around to park on the cabstand. As I sat there, I could see in the window of the beauty parlor across the street. Jessie was working on a lady in the first chair. I couldn't see the lady's face. I wondered if we had found all the spies that were giving Lenny and Kent all that intel on us as we moved around. I made a mental note to keep an eye on Jessie and to let Josie know that it would be worth a look.

At noon, I pulled in front of the Smokehouse. I had picked up a few fares during that morning, but I was not gonna be late for this meeting. When I got to the door of the club, Henry opened it and told me that Josie was in her office. I walked in the door, she was sitting behind her desk, sipping her teacup. She looked at me with her wise, sharp gaze and said, "You have done well by me. I told you that I would pay for the info about my son's killer, and you saw it through." She handed me a wad of bills and said, "This is the five thousand I promised you, now I think you done went above and beyond what we agreed on. So we got one more thing for you. Would you like to run the cabstand, or you could have a numbers book all your own? You choose what you want to do."

I said, "Don't the cabstand belong to Henry?"

She smiled and said, "Henry gonna give up the cabstand, he got bigger and better things to do nowadays."

When I heard that, I told her that I would be glad to run the stand. She then explained how the cabstand worked and how the money I collected went right into my pocket and the only money I had to pay was to split the fee that was charged to any new cabs that were added to the stand. It usually cost a new driver forty bucks to get a regular place on the stand, this money could be made back in a day on the stand. So I thanked her and left the Smokehouse.

Doris and I enjoyed the game that evening, we always wore gray and white to the game because it's the team's colors. A week or two went by, and then we heard the news, there was a fire at Lenny's house one night while the family slept. The house burned to the ground, there were no survivors. A few days later, there was news of a big shootout. The word was that Max Lucci and W. B. Robinson were found dead one morning as the sun came up. It was said that Max was a suspect in the fire at Lenny's house and W. B. was trying to bring him in. Looked like it was a shoot-out between the two.

After that, things were happening fast, I got a call from Eric inviting me and Doris to have dinner at the Smokehouse that next evening. When we showed up, we had decided on wearing brown. When we walked into the room, we got a good table and ordered our food and drinks. Around that time, I took a look around the room, I saw Eric walking by a table were Pap Gaines and his wife sat. As Pap got up to shake his hand, I saw that he was wearing an olive green double-breasted sport coat with gray and olive green plaid slacks, his olive green shoes were very shiny. Later I found out that they were made of eel skin. His hat was gray and made of beaver skin. As Eric moved away from his table, I could see that he too had made a change; the suit he had on had to be tailor-made the way it fit, it was sky blue, his shoes were light blue, and the vest to the suit was the same color as the shoes.

As he walked up to the table, I rose to shake his hand. When I did, he grabbed my hand and waved me back to my seat, he said, "My friend, it's good to see you. I hear you have made a choice and now that you will run the cabstand. I have a few things to offer you as well now that I will be running the numbers here in town and taking over the Kent's real estate business. I have talked to the phone company about putting a couple of phone booths at the corner of the cabstand where people can call for a cab as well as walk up for one. Then if you would like, you can have the phone numbers of the booths printed on the cabs, and speaking of cabs, I have five cars parked out in back here I would like to sell you. These cars could help you start your cab company, if you are interested?"

I nodded my head yes, and before I could ask how much, he said, "I will take one thousand dollars for the five of them. The three Fords are four door and would make great cabs, the Dodge also, but the little Hudson is two-door, maybe not a great cab but a good car for Doris here." He smiled as he said all this, knowing that he and I had talked about the fact that Doris needed her own car to run her errands and go to the beauty parlor that she wanted to.

I told him that sounded like a good idea. He said, "Good because the funeral parlor in Rossville would like to buy that hearse of yours. I told them you wouldn't take less than fifteen hundred for the big car." He smiled again because he knew I only paid a few hundred for the car.

He was a very good listener and had a good mind for business. He told me that the Rossville parlor was hoping to open up a new shop right here in Chattanooga. So the purchase of the hearse would give them that chance. Then he said that he had men that would want to rent the cabs from me and pay their dues to work on the cabstand, and when I got things going, I could open up an office and take both of the phone numbers from the phone booths that were written on the side of the cabs for my office. This would mean that I would have my own cab company, then maybe I could hire Doris to run the office and answer the phone and dispatch the cabs. By now Doris was almost drooling, her eyes went back and forth between us, and when she heard all that, she jumped across the table and gave me a hug and told me to say yes to all that stuff and anything else this man has got to say.

I knew Doris hated the hearse and always wanted it gone, so I nodded my head and shook his hand and told the man that we had a deal. Then he moved on to other news, that he and Simon were in the process of opening up at least three more Piggly Wiggly stores, one in St. Elmo, one in Avondale, and one here in Alton Park. Since I ran the cabstand at his store in Highland Park, I would be his first choice to run the cabstand in front of all those stores and anymore that we will open up. This sounded like a real big deal. I had told Eric about Simon and him about Eric, this would be my reward.

As the night went on, I saw Bean Gaines come in. When I saw him at the bar, he looked me over and nodded his head at my brown suit and my beige shirt and shoes. He told me that he was going by Miss Moody's tailor shop one day this week. "I'll come by the cabstand and see if you out there if you want to join me." He had on a plaid sport coat that was mustard and gray, his pants were gray, and his shoes were mustard and were made of ostrich. The shirt had BEAN written on one cuff and GAINES on the other. His cuff links were mustard and gray, the man was sharp. I told him that I would be there. He put out his hand, and I shook it.

When Doris and I got home, we talked into the night about all our plans. She didn't know what to do about the job offer to help me out with the cabstand or stick with Simon and help him run all the new stores. When we finally went to bed, I told her that I would bring the Hudson over to the store so she could see it and drive it around. We made love and finally drifted off to sleep.

As the days went by, the summer was over. One day when I was in my garden, a car pulled up and blew the horn. I looked up, and it was Sadie May and Maryjo, they were dressed up in their Sunday dresses, they both looked and smelled like heaven to me. I waved hello as I came out to the street where the car was parked. They were both smiling.

Sadie May said, "We just wanted to stop by to say thank you again, Mr. Shang. We are on our way to church, soon I will be starting my new job as a schoolteacher, and Maryjo will return to school."

I looked at Maryjo, who knew that it was not her time to talk, children were only allowed to speak when spoken to, so she nodded her head and remained quiet. Sadie May frowned up a bit like a storm cloud passing across the sun's path on a sunny day. She said, "I wanted to teach at Lincoln High School years ago, but that darn Albert Johnson was the principal, and no woman could get a job there unless she slept with him first, and it won't no other place a colored woman could work. All them years I went to school, All I can say is that when Maryjo gets done with school, I hope it will be way more jobs for folks like us."

I nodded my head and said, "Yeah, I hope so too. It's a dam shame things have been so tight for us."

Then she smiled and said, "Good luck with your cab business." She turned her head to look at all the cars I had sitting in my driveway and on the street.

I said, "Things are going well." As they pulled away, Maryjo waved, and I wondered just what she was studying all the way up in Virginia at that college.

Later on that evening, I saw a car I knew well passed by the house. It was Bean Gaines. He pulled up and got out of the car. I came around the side of the house and met him. He and I were becoming fast friends. He had helped me find and design clothes, and he was a fair hand at auto repair, or I should say maintenance. He told me that he was dropping off James Theodore, he and Maryjo were going to the Ball Park on a date, and if I could drop him off after the game at his grandmother's house in St. Elmo, he would pay the cab fare now. I shook my head at the offer of money, told him I would be glad to.

Then he asked me if I had anybody to drive my cabs yet. I said, "No, but I'm gonna put an ad in the paper."

Bean shook his head, he said, "Man, why don't you let some of them numbers boys take on the cab job. Hell, you blessed and favored by the new king of Alton Park. Ain't a soul in his right mind or his wrong one gonna dare cross you."

I looked at Bean and laughed at what he had to say. Most of them Morton boys got cars, but all them newcomers have a hard time getting around. I thought about it a minute then shrugged and said, "Hell, why not? If they pay the rent on the cab and stand fees, it would be better than having all these pretty cabs just sitting here."

Later that night, I was sitting on my back porch playing with the dog and listening to the game. When it ended, I saw James and Maryjo come across the street from the Ball Park. I told James that I would wait here for him as he walked her home. When he got back to my house, we drove off. As I drove the young man home, he talked about his plans to go to school. He told me that his grandmother had worked for one of the Brooks's family cleaning house and that he was given a job at the factory by Mrs. Brooks to help him earn money to go to school. Now he would join the Army reserve to help him get money using the G.I. Bill. That after WW2, black soldiers were allowed to use the G.I. Bill. I told him that it sounded like a good plan then asked what he would study.

The young man looked at me and said, "One thing for sure, Mr. Shang, it won't be the numbers game." We both laughed at that, and the boy got out of the cab and said thank you.

The next morning, I got a call from Charlie. He told me that he had two men that were looking to rent a couple of the cabs. I told him to have them come by the house. At ten that morning, they were at my door. Both men had their money to pay the rental and the dues to start. I told one man to go by the cabstand at Simon's store in Highland Park, the other would work at the stand on Main Street.

When I pulled up at the cabstand, Melvin ran over to the cab and asked if there was still a cab open. I told him yeah, so he said that he and his brother wanted to rent one of the cabs. I told him okay. Before the week was out, all my cabs were on the stands and working. A month or so later, a building a few blocks down Main Street from the stand became open, it was a small storefront building with a big back room and large bay door; it was big enough to drive two or three cars in to do work on if the weather was bad, and it had a good size parking area to allow me to park all the cabs there. I called Eric to see what he thought about me renting this building and how to get the phone company to hook up the phone from the booths. By this time, those phones would ring night and day. We had to put a bench by the phone booths so we could keep up with it. Eric told me to give him a week.

When he called me that next week, he told me that it was all set. I could sign the lease and move in right away and that the phone would be installed before the week was out. The small store had a desk and a few file cabinets already in place. Soon as I got things going, Doris started coming by in the evening to help me manage the business. She knew how to set up the books and payroll. She helped me set up accounts to get gas at local stations at a discount. Soon I was able to hire a mechanic to help keep the cabs going. With Doris running back and forth from Highland Park to Main Street in Alton Park, she had been noticed by Jessie and her sisters and cousins.

One evening, all four of those ladies came up behind Doris and surrounded her. They started to push and hit her. She managed to pull out the gun she had been carrying. As she raised the gun to fire it, all the ladies ran away, yelling and screaming. She told me that it made quite a seen, people in the parking lot and in the store saw and heard most of what went on. She said that she jumped in her car and drove away before the police came, if they were called. About a week later, Jessie was found dead in the alley near the beauty parlor where she worked. I got a call from Doris from the police station. They were holding her on a manslaughter charge. She was in tears, telling me that she didn't do it, she didn't kill jessie. As good as things were going, now the love of my life was in a world of trouble, so I'm going to have to play detective again.

About The Author

Van Guines currently lives and works in Virginia. He was born in Chattanooga, Tennessee and has always loved the place. *The King of Alton Park* is his first book and is based on a true story. Van has taken the true story of his ancestors and created a larger than life murder mystery. With the city of Chattanooga in 1950 as the backdrop, Van has studied many years to become a mystery writer and is now ready to join the ranks of the more well-known mystery writers, like his favorite authors from the past Lawrence Sanders and John Macdonald. He has found a fresh new character in Shang Butler. He's as colorful and full of danger as most of today's mystery characters like Easy Rawlins or the great Stephanie Plum.

Shang Butler is known to be a brave man. He's known for his bravery on the battlefields of World War 1 to the back streets of the Chattanooga criminal underworld where there is never a dull moment and nothing is cut and dry. The reason for the actual murder of Zeebdee Morton has to this day still not been solved, but *The King of Alton Park* gives it one hell of a spin. These questions about the night he was killed were never answered, why was he across town unarmed, shooting pool in a bar without his crew (the Morton boys)? The man owned five pool halls and was being groomed to be the next king of Alton Park. To this day, these and many other questions are still part of the real-life mystery that this story is based on.

Zebedee Moton 1905- 1941

Tom Moton 1875-1948

Mary Jo Moton 1934-2021

Sara Bell Moton aka Sadie Mae 1911-1991